TANNER: YEAR EIGHT

A TANNER SERIES
BOOK EIGHT

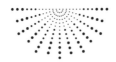

REMINGTON KANE

Year Zero Publishing

INTRODUCTION

TANNER: YEAR EIGHT

Tanner wasn't in love with Tonya Wilson but loved being around her. Like himself, Tonya had a secret she kept hidden. Tanner knew she wasn't the simple personal assistant she claimed to be, and she was aware he was more than an average real estate investor.

Everyone has a secret, and Tanner could live with not knowing Tonya's. But then she died in what the police were calling a "Tragic accident," and Tanner found himself mourning her loss.

But was it an accident, or was it murder? And if murder, what was the reason for it?

More importantly, who killed Tonya Wilson? Who took away yet another person Tanner cared about?

When Tanner went looking for answers, he discovered Tonya's secret and the deadly reason why she was targeted for death.

No. Tanner hadn't been in love with Tonya Wilson, but he'd be damned if he wouldn't avenge her death and make every last person responsible for it pay with their own lives.

It's Tanner on a rampage, and the guilty can run, but they can't hide.

ACKNOWLEDGMENTS

I write for you.

—Remington Kane

FALLING IN LIKE

I'M NOT IN LOVE, TANNER THOUGHT, AND IT WAS TRUE. IT was also true that Tonya Wilson provoked strong feelings from him.

Tonya was twenty-five, and a hot brunette with ocean blue eyes. Tanner felt something whenever he looked into those eyes, something that made him smile.

In love or not, he loved being around her, and the feeling was mutual. They'd met only two weeks earlier. It felt like they had known each other longer.

Tanner had been in New York City after fulfilling a contract in Pennsylvania. Since he was so close to Manhattan, he figured he'd stop there before flying down to Miami. Romeo was planning to fly back to the states, after having been hired to fulfill a contract on a drug dealer in Miami. The drug dealer was currently visiting family in Puerto Rico. A rival dealer was willing to hire Romeo to kill the man when he returned to Miami. Tanner wanted to be in Miami to spend time with Romeo once he had fulfilled his contract.

He hadn't seen Joe Pullo in months and there was always the chance that old Sam Giacconi might have work for him. If it was something simple, he could have the job done and still meet Romeo in Florida.

After arriving late to the city, Tanner got a hotel room, had dinner, then went to bed. He rose early the following morning to go for a run in Central Park. It was summer, 2011, and the city was packed with tourists. By getting to the park early, Tanner could avoid the crowds of tourists and the other runners and walkers who would fill the jogging trails.

As a Tanner, he ran full-out whenever he ran, and would routinely cover ten miles. He'd been motoring along in his fourth mile when a woman joined him on the trail and matched his pace. That she could keep up with him had been impressive. That she continued to do so and finished the ten-mile run alongside him was doubly impressive.

That woman had been Tonya.

They shared smiles along the first few laps they ran together, but then the strain of keeping up with Tanner took away the grin from Tonya's face. As Tanner slowed to signal the end of the run, she made her way over to the grass and collapsed onto her back. She was gulping in air and wiping away sweat.

Tanner had stood nearby. There was a sheen of perspiration on his brow, and he was breathing through an open mouth, but he looked like he could do it all again, which he most certainly could.

When she could speak, Tonya sat up and smiled at him.

"Do you run at that pace every time?"

"I do."

"How many miles did you run?"

"Ten."

"Wow. I usually only run five or six, and not that fast."

"You kept up with me today. Did that tire you out?"

"Hell yeah, it did."

"Let me buy you breakfast. My name is Tanner."

She made it to her feet and stuck out her hand. "I'm Tonya, Tanner. Tonya Wilson."

Tanner took the offered hand and found himself smiling. From that moment on, they had spent every spare minute together.

ALONG WITH HIS ATTRACTION TO HER, TANNER FELT something else. Tonya was lying to him. He'd always been good at detecting lies, with one notable exception. That exception had been a woman he loved, the first woman he'd loved. Her deceit had been monumental and had nearly cost him his life, along with the lives of Romeo and Spenser.

It was because of that he had become wary of love, of romantic love, and distrusted the emotion. As much as he liked her, he was certain he didn't love Tonya. The two times he'd been in love, it had struck him like a brick and taken him over completely. What he felt for Tonya wasn't like that.

Tonya claimed she was a personal assistant to an executive at the corporation she worked at, which was Dangal Corp.

Tanner had heard of Dangal Corp. and knew they were huge and growing throughout the northeast of America. He didn't doubt she worked there, but there was more to it than that. It was something about the way she spoke whenever she mentioned it. Tanner got the impression she regretted having to lie to him. He could understand that. He felt the same way about lying to her.

He had told Tonya he was a real estate investor. That was true enough, as he did have money invested in real estate at various times. He'd recently bought a small house in Nevada that he had renovated and flipped for a profit. If the Feds or the IRS ever questioned him about his source of income, Tanner would be able to account for his spending by the money he made in legal enterprises. Most of the money he made from his illegal ventures was either invested under false identities, stored away in various banks, or given away to good causes.

It was after they had first made love that Tonya began to question him. Tanner was certain she knew he wasn't telling her the whole truth about himself. Being intimate, they touched often. Tonya was aware he always carried a gun.

"For self-protection," he'd told her, but there were other things as well that pointed to him being more than a real estate investor.

"These look like healed bullet wounds," she had said, while she probed his scars delicately with a fingertip. "My uncle was in Vietnam, and he has scars that look like these."

Tanner had told her the truth about some of them, the ones he had gotten when his family was attacked and killed. It shocked him he had told her the truth about that. He rarely spoke of it to anyone.

That attack accounted for the most grievous of his scars but not for all of them, some of which were obviously acquired in recent years.

4

He had changed the subject by asking her to tell him more about her job at Dangal Corp. The look on her face told him she understood he knew she had secrets of her own. After that, they lived with the lies and just enjoyed being around each other.

Tanner would head back to Las Vegas eventually, or so he told himself, but whenever he thought about leaving Tonya behind, he felt a twist in his gut.

No. He was not in love, but he sure as hell liked her.

TANNER'S PLANS TO VISIT FLORIDA HAD FALLEN THROUGH, along with Romeo's contract. Someone had killed the target while he was home in Puerto Rico. The man had gotten fatally stabbed during a bar fight. With Romeo's plans scuttled, Tanner figured he would head back to Las Vegas instead. Not that he was in any hurry to leave New York, not after having met Tonya.

He'd been in the city for two weeks before he finally got around to visiting Sam Giacconi. He'd been hoping to find Pullo as well, as Pullo could often be found at the funeral parlor the old man owned.

Pullo wasn't there. Giacconi wasn't there either, and the funeral parlor was no more.

Cabaret Strip Club, read the sign above the door. Tanner went inside and found a light crowd watching a blonde dance up on stage. It was late afternoon on a workday. The place was bound to get more crowded as men got off work.

A sexy woman with long dark hair approached him and asked him if he'd like to buy her a drink. She was topless; the perky breasts sat up high above her slim waist. Having gotten a closer look at her, Tanner guessed she was no more than nineteen and still a girl. Her "Drink," which would have been only water, would have cost him enough to buy four drinks of good whiskey at a regular bar. Tanner declined her offer of company and her smile disappeared as quickly as it had emerged.

He took a seat at the bar and ordered a beer. The bartender was a middle-aged man with sandy-colored hair and a pleasant face, although his eyes looked sad. He wore a name tag that stated he was Carl. Carl the bartender.

"Does Joe Pullo ever come in here?" Tanner asked. He had to speak loudly to be heard over the music the blonde was dancing to.

Carl said, "I wouldn't know, sir," in a tone that told Tanner he did know. He had also become nervous and was licking lips that had gone dry. Not knowing who Tanner was, Carl had no way of knowing if Tanner was looking for Pullo to do him harm. It was a smart move to deny knowing anything about Pullo.

Tanner faced the bar and looked into the mirror beyond it to take in what was going on behind his back. He could also watch the blonde dance that way. She was good at it, had a slim but shapely body, and was an expert at pole dancing.

Her routine ended, and a woman with dyed red hair took her place. The girl with the long dark hair had found someone to buy her a drink. The guy wasn't much older than she was, had acne scars, and was overweight. It was worth twenty bucks to him to spend a few minutes talking to the topless beauty who smiled at him.

He was in the middle of a sentence when another man walked in and the girl went to make her offer to him. The new guy took her up on it and paid another twenty bucks for a drink for the girl. The girl had made the Cabaret

Strip Club forty bucks during the ten minutes Tanner had been there. Tanner guessed they could pay her two or three hundred dollars a day to drink water and still make money.

He had finished his overpriced beer and was about to leave when Pullo walked in. Carl the bartender called to him.

"This guy was asking about you, Mr. Pullo."

Tanner decided he liked Carl. The man had warned Joe about him in case he meant to be trouble. He took out a twenty and laid it on the bar, as a tip for Carl.

When he saw that Pullo was smiling as he walked over, Carl relaxed.

"You two are friends?"

"This is Tanner, Carl. If he comes in here, put his drinks on my tab."

"Yes sir, Mr. Pullo."

After shaking hands, Pullo gestured for Tanner to follow him. They walked toward the office. It was in the same place it had been when the building housed a funeral parlor. The furniture was different, and a door had been added, one that led out to the alleyway along the side of the building.

Pullo sat on a green leather sofa. Tanner settled near him. With the door closed, the music from the bar was muted enough to talk in a normal voice.

"Did you come here looking for Sam?"

"I did. When did he open a strip club?"

"It's not his. It belongs to Johnny R, Johnny Rossetti. The kid is making a fortune from the place."

"So, Sam is no longer in the funeral business. What's he doing?"

"He still runs things from out of his house. Do you need to see him?"

"I was wondering if he had any work for me. I plan to be in New York for a few more weeks."

"There's nothing right now, but we'll keep you in mind."

"How have you been, Joe?"

"Things are good overall. I'm running a crew of my own now."

"But? I heard a but in there."

Pullo sighed. "Gracie and I are over for good. She met someone else at that compound of hers."

Gracie was Gracie James. Tanner had met her the same time Pullo had, when they had gone to Pennsylvania to kill several men seven years earlier. Gracie was involved with a militia and Pullo was a member of the New York mob. Tanner was surprised their on-again, off-again, long-distance romance had lasted as long as it had.

"It's a shame you won't see her anymore, but I wish her luck. I always liked Gracie."

"Oh, hell yeah. I wish her luck too, and we're still friends."

Tanner stood. He had plans to meet Tonya for dinner. With rush hour in full swing and rain expected to begin at any moment, he would allow himself enough time to reach the restaurant early.

"You taking off?"

"Yeah, I have to meet someone."

"A woman?"

"Yeah."

"Too bad you can't stay a little longer. I would have introduced you to Johnny. The kid is going places, Tanner. He's smarter than I'll ever be."

"I doubt that, Joe. You're pretty damn sharp."

Pullo walked him out of the club through the new side door. Pullo's black Hummer was parked there.

"I'll let Sam know you're back in town and call you if anything comes up."

"Do that," Tanner said.

They shook hands again before Tanner headed to his car. It had begun to rain before he reached it.

2

TEARS IN THE RAIN

THE RAIN WAS COMING DOWN HARD A HALF HOUR LATER, AS Tanner stood beneath the protection offered by the restaurant's green awning.

Tanner had made reservations at a restaurant that he had eaten at before years earlier. Tonya loved Italian food and the restaurant was touted as one of the best in the city. They would have time for drinks before they had to take their table. Tanner was looking forward to giving Tonya a gift he'd bought for her.

Tonya loved jade jewelry. Tanner had seen a jade bracelet in the window of a jeweler he'd been passing that morning and decided to buy it for her. The thing hadn't been cheap, as the stones were set in gold.

He spotted her arriving in her car. It was a red Lexus that was two years old. Tonya had bought the car used, but it was still a pricey automobile. Her apartment was in a modern building with a doorman and many of her clothes bore the labels of well-known fashion designers.

If she was only a personal assistant, she was a highly

paid one. Whatever it was she did at Dangal Corp. rewarded her well.

He watched Tonya as she left her car. She had an umbrella up and was smiling at him after spotting him. There was a car approaching from her left that had its headlights off. It had crept out of a parking space slowly only to speed up. Tonya spotted it and increased her pace to cross the street. When the car was even with her, she pointed at it and yelled to the driver.

"Your lights are off!"

The headlights came on and the car kept going.

Tonya kissed Tanner and pointed at the departing vehicle. "There was a woman behind the wheel of that car and three kids in the back seat. It's no wonder she was too distracted to put on her lights."

They entered the restaurant and took seats at the bar until it was time for their reservation.

"How was work?" Tanner asked.

"It was fine. What about you? This morning, you said you might be working soon."

"That fell through."

"Oh. I hope that doesn't mean you'll be going back to Las Vegas."

Tanner reached over and caressed her cheek. "I'm in no hurry to leave you."

"And how would you feel about taking me with you?"

"You want to live in Las Vegas?"

Tonya leaned in and kissed him. "I want to be wherever you are."

Tanner had clasped her right hand during the kiss. When it ended, he revealed the bracelet he had bought Tonya. Her eyes went wide as she took it in.

"Oh, my God. Is that for me?"

"Do you like it?"

"I love it. Damn, Tanner, you're spoiling me."

"You're worth spoiling."

The bracelet fit Tonya's wrist well, and it matched the gold and jade earrings she had on.

They spoke more over dinner about what the future held for them. Tanner had seen the results of a long-distance relationship by watching Pullo and Gracie. He didn't want the same thing. He didn't want a committed relationship either, but whenever he thought of never seeing Tonya again, it saddened him.

"What happens to your job if you move to Las Vegas?"

Tonya shrugged. "I'd have to quit. I've been thinking about doing so anyway. Things have changed at Dangal Corp. over the last few months. Now is a good time for me to leave."

Tanner was silent.

"Maybe you don't want me to move to Las Vegas. Is that it, Tanner?"

"No. I would love to have you there."

"So, why do you look so sad?"

"We need to have a serious talk before you make such a big move. There are things about me you should know."

"Such as secrets. Like why you always carry a gun?"

"Yes. And you have secrets of your own."

"I do," Tonya admitted.

"Why don't we head back to your apartment and finally have that conversation?"

Tonya nodded, and her eyes had grown moist.

"What's wrong?"

"This could be our last night together once the truth comes out."

"It could be, but we've danced around each other's secrets long enough."

Tonya removed a tissue from her purse and dabbed at

her eyes. "Let's get out of here. We'll talk in private at my apartment."

Tanner paid the bill, and they went outside. If anything, it was raining harder than it had been earlier. Tanner took Tonya in his arms and kissed her.

"My car is parked down the block. I'll meet you at your apartment."

"Okay."

Tanner put on a hat and turned up the collar of his raincoat before stepping out from under the protection of the awning.

He was halfway to his car when he heard the sound of an engine revving. That was followed by a scream and a sickening thump. He turned his head to see a car coming toward him. It was a dark vehicle and there was a hooded figure hunched over the steering wheel. The hood was yellow. High beam headlights came on, blinding him, and then the car was speeding past him.

"Tonya," Tanner said, and he was already running as the word left his mouth.

She was lying in the street looking like a discarded doll. One leg was at an unnatural angle, and her right arm was dislocated. Blood seeped from the back of her skull, after having made a dent in the door of the vehicle she was lying beside.

As he settled on his knees beside her, scattered glints of color caught Tanner's eye. They were bits of jade from her bracelet. It had come apart when her wrist had slammed against the wet pavement.

Tanner took out his phone to call for an ambulance, then felt Tonya's left hand grip his wrist. It seemed remarkable she was still conscious, as the ground beneath her head turned red from the blood she was losing.

"I'll get you help, Tonya. Baby, you're going to be all right."

Her lips parted. "I love yo—" and then she was gone. One instant, Tonya had been looking at him from her blue eyes, and then those eyes became as lifeless as marbles.

A woman ran over. She was Asian and said she was a nurse. Tonya's condition was beyond the skills of any nurse or doctor to cure. She was dead.

"I saw the whole thing. That damn car never slowed down, and it kept going after it hit her."

Tanner had only heard part of what she'd said. He was back on his feet and running. The only thought on his mind was to catch up to the car that had struck Tonya... had killed Tonya. Tanner reached his car, started the engine and went in pursuit.

He was having trouble seeing because of the rain. But there were also tears, tears for a woman who, with her last breath, proclaimed her love for him.

Tanner wiped at his eyes and stepped harder on the gas. Someone needed to die.

3
BLACK OPS CORPORATE STYLE

Tanner came upon a wreck and saw that one of the vehicles was large and black. He pulled to the curb and left his car while reaching for his gun. His only thought was to kill whoever had snuffed out Tonya's life.

As he came closer, his shoulders slumped. Neither of the cars involved in the wreck were the one he had seen. The hit-and-run car had been a Cadillac. Tanner recalled seeing the automaker's emblem. He'd also been staring at the license plate when the headlights had blinded him.

He had not been able to read the whole alpha-numeric combination of the license plate before the glare affected him, but he did know that the New York license plate began with the letters KBG, followed by the number 9.

Tanner spoke to an elderly black man who was seated in a Mercedes. "What happened here?"

"A damn fool ran a red light. I barely hit the brakes in time to miss him when the car behind me slammed into me."

"Was it a dark Caddy?"

"Yeah. I think it was." The old man pointed to the

nearest corner. "That car jumped the curb after it went past me and sideswiped the wall of that building."

Tanner spotted something lying on the ground and walked over to get a good look at it. It was the side-view mirror off the Cadillac. Tanner left it where it was and walked back over to talk to the old man.

"That same car was involved in a hit-and-run accident a few blocks back. Tell the police that. And there's a mirror over there that came off that car."

The other driver had been listening. He was a young white guy who appeared shaken up and had blood running from his nose. His airbag had deployed and smacked him in the face.

"Was anyone hurt during the hit-and-run?"

Tanner said, "Yes," and turned away from them, to get back in his vehicle. He was going to keep looking for the Cadillac.

He gave up the search an hour later and stopped to make an anonymous call. He had to let the police know about the license plate of the Caddy. They would be looking for him, and would expect him to make a statement, to aid them in filling out their damn forms.

To hell with their forms and their procedures. To hell with their laws and their legal system as well.

If they ever caught the driver who killed Tonya, they would coddle him with a free lawyer, a heated cell, and three meals a day.

Tanner wanted nothing more than to kill the son of a bitch. To end their lives as they had ended Tonya's. His tears had ceased flowing, to be replaced by a growing sense of rage.

~

Tonya's family traveled to New York from Wisconsin. Tonya had left behind a mother and two younger brothers. They were taking the body home to be buried.

The newspapers were reporting the incident as a hit-and-run accident. Tanner had doubts about that after the police found the driver of the car. His name was Michael Hallam. He was fifty-two and a former employee of Dangal Corp. who had a history of driving drunk.

Meanwhile, Tonya was being listed as an unemployed waitress. Tanner knew for a fact she had been carrying a key card that would allow her access to Dangal Corp's Manhattan headquarters. He had watched her use it to enter the building once after dropping her off outside.

Whatever secret Tonya had been ready to tell him, it must have concerned her employment. Tonya couldn't give him answers, but there was someone who could.

Rae Houghton opened her apartment door after Tanner rang her bell. Tonya and Tanner had run into Rae once when she was out on a date of her own. Later, Tonya had said that Rae used to work with her at Dangal Corp, but that Rae had recently been fired for stealing. Tonya had stated that she hadn't known Rae well, but that she didn't believe she was foolish enough to risk getting fired by stealing. Tonya thought they had fired Rae for an unknown reason and had used the excuse of theft. She had also mentioned she felt sorry for Rae, who had recently rented an apartment in "That new high rise over by the docks."

Tanner was in that building now and had found Rae's apartment.

"You're Tanner. Did you know that the police were looking for you?"

"Can I come in? I want to talk to you about Tonya."

Rae's face fell as she stepped back to let Tanner enter. "I saw what happened to her on the news. The cops said you were there when it happened."

"I was. Tonya died before she could be helped. What do you know about the man who killed her, Michael Hallam?"

"Not much. I used to see him in the halls sometimes. He was an executive of some type. I didn't know he had been fired until I read about it in the newspaper."

"Did Tonya know him?"

"About as much as I did."

Tanner studied Rae and thought she looked nervous. She was a good-looking woman who was the model type and maybe around twenty-five. When Tanner had first met her, she'd had on heels and was eye-to-eye with him.

The apartment reminded him a little of the one Tonya had lived in. It had a large living room and offered the view of a park. Dangal Corp. paid well. Tanner wanted to know what they had been paying for.

There were cardboard boxes piled near the door, and a bookcase was empty.

"Are you moving?"

"I have to. I can't afford this place anymore, not after losing my job." Rae motioned toward her kitchen. "Would you like coffee?"

"What I want is the truth."

"What do you mean?"

"Tonya was going to tell me what she really did for Dangal Corp. but never got the chance. I have a feeling you can tell me."

Rae nibbled on her bottom lip, then sat on her sofa. The sofa was made of yellow leather and looked almost new. The color matched her curtains. The coffee table in front of the sofa was a carved chunk of Carrara white marble. Tanner guessed the thing had to have set her back at least two grand. Rae followed his gaze and ran her hand over the table. There were several items lying on it, a pack of cigarettes, a gold lighter, a half empty beer bottle, a cell phone, and a pink, plastic cap from something that wasn't in sight.

"This coffee table is nice, isn't it? It weighs a ton, but I just love it. When I was growing up, we were so poor we used those big wooden wire reels for coffee tables. The smaller ones were our chairs."

"Where was that?"

"Over in New Jersey."

Tanner sat beside her. "Tell me about Tonya. What sort of work was she really doing?"

Rae settled back, and the leather made a squeaking sound. "Dangal Corp. has what they call a black ops division. Tonya was one of their corporate spies."

"She infiltrated other companies to learn their trade secrets?"

Rae reached out to grab her cigarettes; as she did so, the sleeve of her blouse rode up her arm, revealing that she had a tattoo. Tanner couldn't make out most of it, just something that looked like an upside-down triangle colored red.

After getting a cigarette lit, Rae continued.

"Tonya and I did more than learn trade secrets, Tanner. Are you sure you want to hear this?"

"Keep talking."

"We would get hired as executive assistants in some places. In others, we would get jobs in the mailroom. A lot of sensitive material passes through a company's mailroom."

"What are you leaving out?"

"What do you mean?"

"So far, nothing you said sounds so bad. I'm sure it's illegal, but I don't think Tonya would have been nervous about telling me this, and she was nervous. Why is that?"

"A new manager took over the black ops division about ten months ago. His name is Brent Hayward. Hayward didn't think our ops were black enough. Instead of working at a company for months hoping to overhear something important or make a copy of a key document, Hayward wanted us to learn how to be better thieves. Tonya and I, along with a few others were put through a course he set up. They taught us how to pick locks, open safes, and even drug people. With those skills, we were bringing back secrets in record numbers. And yeah, if we'd been caught by the cops, we would have all gone to prison for a long time."

"What about sex?"

Rae raised an eyebrow and looked Tanner over. "You want to know if Tonya slept with anyone to find out a corporate secret or two?"

"Did she?"

"No. Hayward brought in pros to do that. Real call girls. They would pick up an executive in a bar, slip him a drug, then take him up to a hotel room. There would be someone else in the hotel who would give the guy a different drug after he passed out, some sort of truth serum. By the time morning came, the guy would have spilled every secret he knew."

"And involve the cops once they left the hotel."

"No. I was told they would have no memory of what happened. If they remembered anything odd, they would probably think it was a dream. When they did wake up, the hooker was in bed beside them and their money was still in their wallets. Their biggest concern was wondering what story to tell their wives about why they had been out all night."

"What other changes were there?"

"Hayward hired these ex-cons, Kevin and Kelly. I heard they had served time for armed robbery. There's a rumor that their job is to help frame people who work for other corporations. And then, there were all the accidents."

"What accidents?"

"A bunch of executives at other companies began suffering fatal accidents, like car wrecks, drowning, or falls down stairs. I heard one guy was electrocuted in his own pool. That executive had been a young guy with a wife and three small kids."

"Who was causing those accidents?"

"I don't know. Maybe they really were accidents, but there were a lot of them."

"Why wasn't Tonya listed as working for Dangal Corp?"

"We couldn't be tied to the company in any official way. If we were ever caught, they could deny everything. The cops only spoke to me because Tonya had my number on her phone."

"Let me have your number. I may have more questions for you over the next few days."

Rae gave it to him, then asked a question. "What are you planning to do?"

"I'm going to find out who killed Tonya. If it's Hallam, he'll pay for it."

"I told Tonya she should have quit before something bad happened to her, but I never thought she would die."

"Tonya was thinking of quitting and moving to Las Vegas with me. I think she would have done so for a fresh start, as much as to be with me. What else are you not telling me?"

Rae sighed. "A man died about a week ago. He was found dead in a hotel room. There was a call girl in the bed beside him. The guy died because he had a reaction to the drug he'd been given... the hooker had been shot. Tonya called and told me about that. She was wondering if the hooker had been one of the girls Hayward hired."

"And she was killed to keep her from talking? Do you think Hayward would have done that?"

"I wouldn't put anything past him. Along with the hookers, Hayward has been hiring violent ex-cons. I don't know what he has them doing, but it couldn't be good."

"And if Tonya had found out something she shouldn't have, Hayward might have had her killed."

Rae wiped at her eyes. "That's what I keep thinking. Michael Hallam claims he's innocent and that someone used his car that night, and then placed it back in his garage."

"What's his alibi?"

"He had none. He was home by himself and drunk. The man is an alcoholic. It's why he lost his job."

Tanner turned and opened the apartment door.

"Where are you going?"

"I'm going to talk to Michael Hallam and get the truth. The paper printed his address."

"If he did run down Tonya; he might have been too drunk to remember."

"He'll still pay for it," Tanner said, and went off to get the truth.

4

EYEWITNESS

YONKERS IS A CITY ON THE HUDSON RIVER IN Westchester County that is bordered by the Bronx. It's about a forty-minute drive from the heart of Manhattan. Over two hundred thousand people call the Yonkers area home. Michael Hallam was one of them.

Hallam's house was on a road off the main drag. The street was hilly, as was much of the city. Hallam's home was white, had two floors, and looked to contain about four bedrooms. Given the area it was in, the home was expensive.

Tanner drove past it once and took a look around the neighborhood. The streets were quiet since it was a weekday. Most of the kids would be in school and their parents at work. He only saw one woman pushing along a baby carriage.

He approached Hallam's home from the rear after scaling a six-foot fence. There was a wooden deck at the rear of the home, along with a yard full of overgrown grass. The grass at the front of the house was high as well. Hallam was a drunk, or he wouldn't have been arrested more than once on DUI charges. Drunks didn't take care of themselves or the things they owned.

After picking the lock on a rear door, Tanner saw that the inside of the home was just as messy. There were take-out cartons and pizza boxes in the living room and the kitchen, along with numerous empty whiskey bottles.

The story in the paper had mentioned that Hallam's wife had left him after his last DUI arrest. She should have taken the damn car when she went. If Hallam hadn't had access to a vehicle, Tonya might still be alive.

The TV was on in the living room, but it had been muted. After checking upstairs and finding no one there, Tanner went back down the stairs. He was considering waiting for Hallam to return home when he noticed an open doorway that was beside the door that led to the deck. When he walked over, he saw a set of stairs leading down to the basement.

"Mr. Hallam! Are you down there? This is the police, Mr. Hallam."

No one answered, and then Tanner caught the scent. It was a coppery odor mixed with feces. He went down the stairs with his gun out and found what he thought he might.

Hallam was dead. He had a single gunshot wound on the right side of his head at the temple. The body was lying on the floor of the basement and there was a gun beside it. Judging by the blood, it appeared that he'd been dead for hours.

Tanner's first thought was that the man had committed suicide, but as his eyes studied the scene, he knew he was looking at a murder. Two things pointed toward it. One was obvious, while the other was merely suggestive.

Hallam wore his watch on his right wrist, something many left-handed people did, and yet, he had been shot in the right temple. That could be nothing. Maybe he just liked wearing his watch on that wrist. And then there were his hands. Hallam's hands were clasped together loosely. Had he shot himself, he would not have been able to join his hands together afterwards.

Those joined hands might have been Hallam pleading for his life. If so, his murderer had shown no mercy.

Someone had killed Hallam and wanted it to look like a suicide. That someone was covering up something. They might also be the one who was really driving Hallam's car on the night Tonya was killed.

Tanner searched the house, including Hallam's personal files, but left everything as he'd found it. Hallam had worked for Dangal Corp. for more than twenty years before being fired. His wife of thirty-one years had left him, and he had been accused of killing a woman while driving drunk. Trying to make people believe the man had committed suicide would not be a hard sell.

Tanner left the house the way he had entered and returned to his car. If Hallam couldn't give him the answers he needed, maybe he would find them inside Dangal Corp.

HOMICIDE DETECTIVE COLLEEN BLUM WAS CALLED TO Hallam's home less than an hour after Tanner had left it. Hallam's estranged wife had discovered his body in their basement.

Blum had come to the same conclusion Tanner had and for the same reasons. Hallam had indeed been left-handed, and those clasped hands gave the lie to the notion of suicide.

Detective Blum was fifty-one, attractive, smart, and had

become jaded by her work and having to deal with the bureaucracy of the New York City Police Department and people in general.

She had initially believed Tonya Wilson's death was a simple hit-and-run caused by a drunk driver, but with Hallam's murder, doubt had crept in. She'd already had questions, such as how an unemployed waitress like Tonya could afford a luxury car and a high rent apartment. Because of Tonya's good looks, she believed the woman might have been the property of a sugar daddy. That didn't seem to be the case. Neighbors said she had rarely been seen with anyone but that lately she had been in the company of a man with "Some serious eyes," as many had described him. Blum later learned that Tonya's boyfriend was named Tanner. Whether that was a first name or a last name, she didn't know.

Tanner had been at the Italian restaurant with Tonya on the night she was killed. A check of the restaurant showed that he paid the bill with cash, so, there was no luck tracking him down through a credit card.

The Tanner mystery aside, along with the riddle of where Tonya's money came from, there was now this murder of her alleged killer.

Michael Hallam had vehemently denied having driven anywhere on the night Tonya was killed. Blum had found herself believing him. She sure as hell believed him now that someone had silenced him.

A call had come in that night anonymously. The caller had given them the description of Hallam's vehicle, most of the numbers and letters from the license plate, and had stated that the driver had been wearing a yellow hoodie. They found the car all right, but a search of Hallam's home hadn't turned up a yellow hoodie. That had bothered Blum. If the man was trying to cover up his crime, why keep the car but get rid of the jacket you were wearing? That didn't make sense.

Something was going on that had so far led to the deaths of two people. The Yonkers Police Department would handle Hallam's murder. As far as Tonya's case went, Blum's captain was pressuring her to close the case and label it a hit-and-run.

Blum wasn't willing to do that yet. While it was possible Hallam had killed Tonya during a drunken drive through the city, and then later been killed for an unrelated reason, her instincts were saying different. The two cases were linked somehow.

She had said goodbye to the Yonkers' detectives handling the case and was walking toward her car when a girl approached her. The child was about thirteen, was cute, had long hair, and was in a wheelchair.

"Are you a police detective?"

"I am. I'm Detective Blum. How may I help you, young lady?"

"I'm Heidi. I saw the man who killed Mr. Hallam."

Blum removed the card the Yonkers detective had given her and took out her phone to call him.

"I want to hear what you have to say, Heidi, but there are others who need to hear it too."

"Okay. But I only saw the man from behind. I was looking out my window when he was at Mr. Hallam's front door."

Blum had dialed the number on the card but hadn't pressed the call button yet. She asked Heidi what the man she saw looked like.

"He was tall, and kinda skinny, I guess."

"Was he white? Black? And what about his hair color?"

"I don't know. I only saw him from behind and he was wearing a yellow hoodie."

"A yellow hoodie? Are you certain?"

"Um-hmm. After watching Mr. Hallam let him inside the house, I went back to getting ready for school. When I came home, I heard that Mr. Hallam had been killed. Am I right? Did I really see the killer?"

"Yes, honey. I think you did."

Blum made her call and remained in Yonkers for another three hours.

5
DIGGING DEEPER

Tanner spoke with Rae again, over the telephone. He needed a place to start inside Dangal Corp. and Rae knew the players.

She told him about a young man named Dustin Evans. Evans was a member of Dangal Corp's black ops division and a corporate spy.

"Dustin is sexy as hell and has curly blond hair. He gets the executive assistants to tell him all kinds of secrets, and he'll sleep with them too, even the married ones."

"What was his relationship with Tonya?"

"They had none. She didn't like him, but I went out with him. That was a big mistake."

"Why?"

"He dumped me as soon as I slept with him. I also think it was Dustin who set me up to be fired for theft. We each had these little cubicles at Dangal Corp. Files were found in my desk one day and I was accused of working as a double agent. Do you believe that? Here's Dangal Corp. training us to steal and disrupt other companies and then they get pissed when they thought someone might be doing the same to them. I didn't take those files, but someone told me they had seen Dustin hanging around my cubicle the day before they were found."

"Do you think he did it on his own?"

"No. That asshole, Brent Hayward, had him do it. Hayward never liked me."

"Did Dustin know that Michael Hallam had been arrested for drunk driving?"

"Everyone knew. Hallam had been high up in the company. It was a surprise when they canned him, drunk driving or not."

"Michael Hallam is dead. Someone killed him and tried to make it look like a suicide."

There was silence on the line, then Rae asked a question.

"Did you kill him, Tanner?"

"No. And I don't think he was driving the car on the night Tonya was killed."

"Why do you think someone tried to make Michael's death look like a suicide?"

Tanner told her his reasons, and she was silent again. Then, once more, she had a question.

"Do you think Tonya was killed on purpose?"

"Yes."

"Damn."

"Yeah."

"Call me anytime, and I'll help you if I can."

"I'll do that. And Rae, watch your back. I don't know what's going on, but it might involve you somehow, since you worked at Dangal Corp. and were a friend of Tonya's."

"I'll be careful, and you do the same."

Tanner ended the call and went looking for Dustin Evans.

∼

RAE OPENED HER DOOR TWENTY MINUTES LATER AND found Detective Blum looking at her.

"May I come in, Ms. Houghton? I have a few questions for you."

"About what?"

"About your friend, Tonya Wilson. I need to know more about her."

"Tonya and I weren't that close."

"You still knew her. Tell me, how did she make her living?"

Rae shrugged. "She had a bunch of different gigs, I guess. You know how it is in this city. One job doesn't pay the bills for most people, and you have to hustle."

"I can't find any source of employment for Ms. Wilson. I mean legitimate employment. The same is true for you, but you live here in a fancy apartment. How is that, Ms. Houghton?"

Rae crossed her arms over her chest. "Should I call a lawyer?"

Blum held up a hand. "I'm not here to cause you grief. I'm trying to find out who killed your friend."

"I thought it was Michael, Michael Hallam?"

"I no longer believe that. He's been murdered as well."

Rae pretended to be hearing that news for the first time. "How was he killed?"

"Someone staged a suicide, but it was murder."

"Wow. And you think Tonya was murdered too?"

"Yes. That's why I need your help. Tell me about Tonya. Where did her money come from? Was she a call girl? Are you?"

"No. I'm not a hooker and neither was Tonya. We

33

worked for Dangal Corp. as corporate spies. That's where the money came from."

"Dangal Corp? That's interesting."

"Why?"

"There's the fact that Michael Hallam used to work there. I also heard something else concerning them recently from a... friend of mine. But go on, tell me more about what they're doing."

"I don't think I should without getting a lawyer involved. I know the penalties for corporate espionage."

"It is a federal crime, but I swear I'm not after you. I'm after whoever killed your friend."

Rae shook her head. "I can't risk it. And I'll deny I ever said anything to you if you drag me into a police station."

Blum was tempted to do just that, then she thought better of it. Rae was her only source into what was going on. She needed to win her trust.

"I told you I wasn't here to give you grief, and I meant that. Thank you for telling me as much as you have. I think you've pointed me in the right direction. I may call you if I have more questions."

"I've said all I want to say, and I hope you find Tonya's killer."

"I hope so too," Blum said.

She left Rae's apartment building and received a call. She was to go to the scene of a triple homicide in Midtown; her partner was already there.

Blum cursed. With three fresh bodies to deal with, it was a certainty she'd be told to label Tonya's death a hit-and-run accident. And so far, she couldn't prove otherwise.

That didn't mean she was ready to let things go, not after learning about Dangal Corp's connection to the victim.

Blum made a call as she drove toward Midtown.

"This is Thaxton," said a voice.

"Richard, it's Colleen. I want to see you soon. I have something that will interest you."

"Like what?"

"It involves Dangal Corp."

"Let me guess. Someone else is dead?"

"Two bodies. One is a case of mine, and the other is up in Yonkers but connected. I think my case will soon be ruled an accident, but I don't believe it was one."

"And you're hoping I'll keep digging for you? You know, I get paid for what I do, the same as you."

"I also know you can't resist solving a mystery and that you hate people getting away with murder."

"Right on both counts. Those are two reasons I left the job to become a PI. When do you want to meet?"

"Tonight, if possible, but it could be late. I just caught a triple homicide."

"I'll be at Maury's Place tonight. They stop serving food at ten. If you can't get there by then, call and we'll make new plans."

"I think I'll make it, and Maury's has the best steaks in town."

"You're right, and I'll see you later."

"Thank you, Richard."

"Uh-huh."

Blum ended the call and felt better about things. She might be forced to stop looking into Tonya's death, but Richard Thaxton wouldn't stop until he discovered the truth. He was the most stubborn man she had ever known, and her ex-husband.

Blum didn't know it, but someone else was looking into Tonya Wilson's death. His name was Tanner.

6

PRETTY BOY

RAE HAD TOLD TANNER WHERE HE COULD FIND DUSTIN Evans. The man liked to hang out at a bar that was near the headquarters of Dangal Corp.

The bar was pleasant, drew a young crowd, had an old-fashioned jukebox, and there was a small stage where local bands could strut their stuff. There were no bands playing currently but the jukebox filled the space with music. A smaller section was at the rear and contained a set of pool tables. That was where Tanner first spotted Dustin.

Rae said that young Dustin did well with women; it was easy to see why. He was in good shape, but not overly muscular, had blue eyes, and curly blond hair. Dustin had caught the attention of a trio of women who were seated at a table. Two of them were blonde and the other one had dark hair that hung in a single braid down her back. One of them sent the young man a drink.

When Dustin saw that all three women were good-looking, he decided to join them at their table. What followed was a lot of drinking, laughter, and flirting. After two hours of that, Dustin and the woman with the dark braid left the table and headed out into the night.

Tanner followed. He wondered if they were headed to another bar or to a hotel. It turned out to be neither, as they took a cab to the apartment building Dustin lived in. Rae had given him the address and the apartment number.

It was a seventy-year-old building, the type that still had the old metal fire escape. Many of the residents had converted the fire escape landings into balconies, although they overlooked an alley. Most of them had small table and chair sets out on them; however, the one on the sixth floor, which was also the top floor, was filled with plants. Someone was growing tomatoes there.

Tanner used a dumpster to assist his climb onto the first landing on the second-floor, and then onto the one above it. That one was directly outside Dustin's third-floor apartment, and as Tanner discovered, granted a view inside the bedroom.

Before turning away, he'd caught a glimpse of Dustin's pale white buttocks rising and falling as he pleasured the woman with the long braid. Tanner took a seat in a white plastic chair and waited for the fun and games to end, as they always did.

He gave it fifteen minutes before peeking through a corner of the window again. Sure enough, the woman was dressing, and Dustin was lying in bed with a satisfied smile.

After hearing a door shut three minutes later, Tanner took a position to the left of the window and used a ring he was wearing to tap on the wall. It didn't make a loud noise, and he would pause for several seconds before resuming. As he hoped, Dustin had grown curious about what could be making the sound. He appeared at the window to look out. Tanner pressed himself tightly against the wall, keeping just out of sight.

Dustin's face left the window. Tanner tapped again. Stopped, then tapped. Driven by curiosity, Dustin unlocked the window and flung it open. Tanner came into view and ducked through the open window to step inside the apartment. He had his gun out.

"What the hell is this? Are you robbing me?"

Dustin was wearing a pair of red boxer shorts. The room smelled musky and the scent of the woman's perfume was in the air. Tanner gave him a shove and Dustin fell back onto the bed.

"Someone at Dangal Corp. is responsible for the death of Tonya Wilson. What do you know about that, Dustin?"

"What do I...who the hell are you?"

Tanner sent out a kick that landed on Dustin's nose. He held back from putting too much force behind it but still heard the crunch of the cartilage as the nose broke. Blood began dripping onto Dustin's chest as he scrunched his eyes shut and cried out from the sharp pain.

"I ask the questions, Dustin. You answer them truthfully or there will be more pain."

"I think you broke my nose. God, it hurts like a motherfucker."

"Imagine how much a broken leg would hurt. Tell me what you know about Tonya Wilson's death."

"I-I heard she was killed in a hit-and-run accident."

"And I heard there are people at Dangal Corp. who arrange accidents."

Dustin shook his head while holding his nose. "That's not me. And I don't know anything about that."

"What do you know?"

"There's these guys, Kevin and Kelly, they're cousins. They were hired to do setups."

"What do you mean by setups?"

"You know, they do frame jobs. Most of these

companies have moral clauses. They'll make sure an executive at a rival company gets caught with drugs, or maybe a male hooker. That sort of thing."

"And maybe they frame someone for killing a woman while everyone thinks he was driving drunk, hmm?"

"You're talking about Hallam? No way. That guy was really a drunk. And why would anyone want to kill Tonya?"

"Someone killed her, and it wasn't Hallam. Tell me more about this Kevin and Kelly."

"They're both gingers, and they're ex-cons too. They served ten years in a maximum-security prison for an armed robbery. I never talked to them, but you hear things."

"Where can I find them?"

"I don't know. I don't hang out with them. Oh wait. Kevin likes to wear T-shirts all the time. A few of them have the name of a bar on them. Bloke's Bar in Brooklyn. Maybe he hangs out there."

Dustin's hand fell away from his nose as he reached for a wad of tissues from the box on the nightstand. Tanner saw the thoughtful look on his face.

"You've thought of something else. What is it?"

"The angels."

"What angels?"

"Lucifer's Angels. They're a motorcycle gang. I think Hayward uses them sometime to… eliminate people."

"I was told by someone that executives at other companies had died in fatal accidents. Is that the work of the motorcycle gang?"

"I don't know, man. I don't know what they're doing. I do know that Brent Hayward has hired them more than once."

"Where do I find the motorcycle gang?"

"How the hell would I know?"

"Tell me about Brent Hayward. What kind of protection does he have around him?"

"You mean like bodyguards?"

"Yeah."

"There are none. He's a corporate guy. He leaves the dirty work for other people and gives out orders through a guy named Archer. If any of this shit ever went to court, I'd bet that no one but Archer could testify against Hayward. Everyone gets their assignments from James Archer."

"Tell me everything you know about them, and Kevin and Kelly too."

Dustin did so. After rattling off facts and rumors for three minutes, he seemed surprised by how much he knew.

"Are you going after them next?"

"I'm going to talk to anyone who might have had something to do with Tonya's death."

"You knew her, didn't you?"

"I did."

"She was such a hot piece of ass. I so wanted to tap that, but she would always turn me—"

Dustin stopped talking as Tanner kicked him in the face again, then again, and again. He hadn't liked the way he had spoken of Tonya.

The last kick had rendered Dustin unconscious and broken three teeth. Tanner figured when his face finally healed, he wouldn't be quite the pretty boy he had been.

He left the apartment through the door instead of the window. He was off to find Kevin and Kelly.

7

HELP WITH THE CASE

DETECTIVE COLLEEN BLUM ENTERED MAURY'S TAVERN and saw her ex-husband seated at the bar. He was talking to a middle-aged blonde who seemed to be hanging on his every word. The blonde had to be forty-five if she were a day, but the short skirt and multicolored blouse she wore would be more suitable for a woman half her age. A quick spike of jealousy passed through Blum, which she stifled. She and Richard Thaxton had been divorced for twice as long as they had been married. It didn't make sense to be jealous when seeing him with other women.

Thaxton was fifty-five and was one of those men who aged well. He hadn't gained an ounce, was as handsome as ever, and his white temples gave him an air of sophistication.

Blum had fifteen pounds she couldn't seem to lose no matter how often she jogged, crow's feet, and instead of a luminous white, her hair was gaining dull gray strands with each passing birthday.

When Thaxton noticed her walking toward him, he ignored the blonde and stood to give Blum a hug. They might be divorced, but they were still good friends. They had also been bed partners occasionally, when neither one was involved with someone else.

The blonde pointed at Blum. "Who's she?"

"This is Colleen. Colleen, meet Deidre."

"It's nice to meet you," Blum said, not meaning it.

Deidre mumbled something similar.

"I need to speak with Colleen about business, Deidre. I'll stop by your shop when I get a chance, and we'll talk some more."

Deidre stood and gave Thaxton a kiss on the lips. "Make sure you do that." After giving Blum a less than pleasant look, Deidre left the bar.

"What sort of shop does she have?"

"Deidre owns a boutique and caters to the younger set."

"That explains the way she's dressed."

"She does have the body for it though."

"I hadn't noticed. By the way, you have lipstick on your mouth."

Thaxton grabbed a napkin and wiped away all traces of Deidre. He then asked Blum if she was hungry.

"I'm starving. I hope they're still serving dinner."

"It's mostly bar food after nine, but they'll make you a steak if I ask them."

"Then please ask, along with a house salad."

A bartender came over. Blum ordered a white wine and Thaxton asked if they would be kind enough to make Blum a steak, and to cook it well done. The bartender was explaining that they had stopped serving food, when the owner, Maury, called to her.

"Thaxton gets anything he wants, Grace. That man saved my son's life."

It was true. Maury's son had been kidnapped. While

working a different case, Thaxton had come across the house where the kidnappers were keeping their victim. He'd been looking in a window when he heard someone begging for their life. That had been Maury's then sixteen-year-old son, Maury Jr.

One of the kidnapper's had stabbed him and was about to stab him again when Thaxton shot the man through the window. His accomplice ran away and was later captured by the police. Thaxton had kept pressure on Maury Jr.'s stab wound until help arrived and was credited with saving his life. The kidnappers had already provided proof of life to the parents and weren't keen about leaving behind a witness who could identify them. If Thaxton hadn't been there, Maury Jr. would have wound up in a shallow grave, one that the kidnappers had made him dig himself.

"Thanks, Maury. Colleen had to work late and is famished."

Maury waved to Colleen. "Nothing's too good for you either, Detective. The steak is on the house."

"I can't accept that. Someone in the department might think it's a bribe."

"A bribe for what?" Maury said, but he understood. Maury Jr. had gone on to become a cop himself and worked on Long Island.

Blum and Thaxton settled at a table with their drinks. As usual, Thaxton was drinking beer.

Thaxton leaned back in his seat and studied his ex-wife. "What's wrong?"

"Who says anything is wrong?"

"C'mon, Colleen. You know I could always read you like a book."

She sighed. "The captain has decided to close the case on the hit-and-run victim."

"But you don't think it was a hit-and-run."

"I don't. I think it was murder. But why the woman was murdered, or by whom, I have no idea."

"And this concerns Dangal Corp.?"

"Yes."

"Start from the top and tell me everything."

Blum did just that, beginning with her arrival on the scene of Tonya's death on that rainy night and ending with her last conversation with her captain.

"I tried to explain to him there was a connection between Tonya Wilson's death and Hallam's phony suicide in Yonkers, but he just wouldn't listen."

"Let me guess. The clearance rate on homicides has dropped again."

"It's way down, and so are the number of experienced homicide detectives we have working now. The precinct had two more old-timers retire last year. And not to badmouth the new people, but they just don't have the experience needed to solve some of the cases we're seeing. Add to that the increase in gang deaths due to turf wars, and it's no wonder the numbers are down."

"So, if your captain can categorize a death as an accident instead of a homicide, and blame it on a dead drunk, so much the better, and the truth be damned."

"That's a harsh way to put it, but accurate."

"And that's where I come in?"

"I know you were looking into Dangal Corp. because of that other case you had. I thought you might have more luck uncovering something than I would."

Months earlier, Thaxton had a client who had hired him to find out the truth about his wife's death. The wife had been found shot to death in a hotel room by an alleged lover, a man she worked closely with at a competitor of Dangal Corp.

The client swore his wife was faithful and was not having an affair with her subordinate. Thaxton had come away believing the husband may have been right but had been unable to prove a negative, that the affair never happened. It had seemed unlikely the young subordinate, Scott Brown, would have had an affair with his older boss, or that he would have committed a murder suicide. Scott Brown had been engaged to his high school sweetheart, and the wedding was only weeks away when he died.

The dead woman, Fawna Davis, had been the head of corporate security where she was employed. At the time of her death, she'd been working on discovering who had been guilty of a severe data breach concerning their research and development department. Thaxton had learned that Fawna had suspicions that the Dangal Corp. had infiltrated their company with corporate spies. She had been working on proving that allegation before involving federal authorities.

After her death, all files concerning that investigation had gone missing.

"I came away from that investigation frustrated as hell. As much as I tried, I couldn't connect Dangal Corp. to those murders."

"And you're certain they were murders?"

"I am. My gut tells me so. Fawna Davis was devoted to her husband and dedicated to her career as well. I couldn't see her risking both for a romp in bed with Scott Brown. Brown was a good-looking kid, but he was engaged to be married and was religious. He'd spent the summer before the murders in a poor African village helping to dig wells and clear land for farming. A kid like that doesn't decide to start boffing his forty-three-year-old boss, even if she is attractive, as Fawna Davis was. Fawna Davis was also a devout

47

Catholic from a very religious family. The circumstances surrounding her death have rocked her family, although no one believes it's the truth, especially her husband."

"I believe you. How far did you get before you ended the investigation?"

"I never ended it. I told the client, Kyle Davis, that I would keep working on it whenever I could, at no charge. He can pay me what he thinks it's worth when I find out who killed his wife."

"What's your theory?"

"I think Fawna Davis and Scott Brown were murdered by someone riding a motorcycle. I tracked down a witness who said he heard a motorcycle leaving the motel parking lot seconds after the gunshots woke him up. There was also a guy who worked the night shift in a donut shop across the street who claimed to see a "Biker type" hanging around the motel."

"That could have been another guest."

"I know. It's not much. But it's something, or it could turn out to be something. I also developed a source inside Dangal Corp. I think I'll contact her and see if she's got anything new to tell me."

Blum shared details of Tonya's death and the investigation. Thaxton was the only one outside the department she would trust with such information. She thought it was necessary for him to know as much as possible.

"The boyfriend, this Tanner, why is he so hard to find?"

Blum sighed. "I don't know. He must have a reason for avoiding the police. I also think he was the one who left the anonymous message which gave us most of the car's license plate number."

"That doesn't sound like he had anything to do with her death."

"I agree. I was wondering if he might have been the one to kill Michael Hallam, until the eyewitness stated that the man she saw had a slim build and was wearing a yellow hoodie. Everyone I've spoken to who had seen Tanner said he was built like an athlete. And oh yeah, they all mentioned how intense his eyes are."

Blum's steak arrived and their conversation paused as she began cutting her meat. Thaxton helped himself to the fries the steak came with, since Blum didn't want them.

After swallowing one, Thaxton made a statement. "I'll do my best to find Tonya Wilson's killer."

Blum smiled at him, then leaned across the table and kissed him. "Thank you. You never let me down."

Thaxton stared at her. "Remind me. Why did we get divorced?"

"We were working so much back then that we hardly ever saw each other. We both agreed it was better to separate and remain friends rather than become bitter and resent each other."

Thaxton sighed. "I wish we had toughed it out. I miss having you around sometimes."

"I don't have any regrets, and a marriage certificate wouldn't change how I feel about you."

"That's true enough. Do you have any vacation time coming?"

"Are you kidding? I haven't been on a vacation since we took that trip to Mexico four years ago."

"Why don't we make plans to go to Las Vegas and see a few shows?"

"What about Deidre? Aren't you dating her?"

"We're not dating, and we won't be if you agree to go to Vegas with me."

Blum grinned. "I'll go. It could be a few weeks before I get the time off approved."

Thaxton reached over and took her hand. "Great. And maybe we'll take in a Grand Canyon tour too. I've always wanted to see that big hole in the ground."

Blum squeezed her ex-husband's hand. They might be divorced, but they still loved each other. She took the first bite of her steak. It was delicious.

8
KEVIN AND KELLY

WHEN DUSTIN MENTIONED THAT KEVIN AND KELLY HAD served hard time during a ten-year sentence, Tanner had expected the two cousins to be brutes. But both men had normal builds and were five-nine or five-ten. They might have served time, but they had stayed away from the weights while doing so.

Dustin had said they were redheaded. Tanner spotted them within seconds after entering Bloke's Bar in Brooklyn. The bar was crowded, and catered to the blue-collar type, many of whom were dock workers. Tanner blended in while wearing jeans and a leather jacket.

Kevin and Kelly were seated at a table near the rear of the bar. They were talking up two women who might be sisters, since they looked alike. They were cute, had long auburn hair, and were about the same ages as Kevin and Kelly, who were around forty. Neither woman was in the same class as the one Dustin had taken home earlier, but then, Kevin and Kelly weren't as good-looking as Dustin had been. The cousins resembled each other. Along with the dark red hair, Kevin and Kelly both had prominent noses, thin lips, and cleft chins.

Tanner heard one of the women call the man to her right Kevin as he was walking past their table on the way to the restrooms. Kevin's hair was a little longer than his cousin's hair, and his eyes were blue, where Kelly had green eyes.

Tanner was in and out of the bathroom in less than a minute. During that time, Kelly had gone to the bar to grab a fresh pitcher of beer. Tanner bumped into him as he was paying, then pretended to be a clumsy but friendly drunk.

"Whoa. Sorry there, pal. My bad."

"All right, but be more careful there."

"Absolutely."

Kelly moved away from the bar after placing his wallet back inside his pocket. While the wallet had been open, Tanner had read the address on his driver's license. He'd also caught the Boston accent when Kelly spoke.

He left the bar and returned to his car. Kevin and Kelly left about an hour later with the two women. It looked to Tanner like the men would be getting lucky, as the women were hanging all over them.

Kevin drove a blue Honda Accord. One of the women joined him in the front as his cousin and the other woman climbed into the rear.

When they took off and made a turn that took them away from the address Tanner had seen in Kelly's wallet, Tanner assumed they were going to wherever the women lived. It turned out to be an apartment that was only a few blocks away.

The two couples left the car and headed inside the building. When a light came on in a third-floor apartment,

Tanner saw one of the women lower a shade. It looked like the boys would be occupied for a while.

He headed to the address he had seen on Kelly's license. While he had the time, he could search their apartment.

THE COUSINS LIVED TOGETHER IN A TWO-BEDROOM apartment in Brooklyn that was a short drive from the bar. The place was so neat that Tanner wondered if they hired a cleaning service. He found no evidence of that while looking through copies of their bank records that were kept in a file drawer. He did find the compact pistol that was secured to the bottom of that same drawer. Further searching uncovered a second weapon taped to the backside of the headboard on Kevin's bed. They were horrible hiding places. Any experienced cop or parole officer would have found those guns within minutes while searching.

What he didn't find was a yellow hoodie like the one the driver of the car that hit Tonya had been wearing. He hadn't expected to. While he hadn't gotten a look at the driver's face and his view through the window had been distorted by the rain, he was certain the driver of the car had been thinner than either Kevin or Kelly.

Surprisingly, Kevin and Kelly were official employees of Dangal Corp, according to paperwork Tanner found. They were both thirty-nine, had been born only three days apart, and shared the same surname of Doyle.

The corporation had hired them under a state program that reimbursed the corporation half of the cousins' stated salary. It was to encourage businesses to hire ex-cons.

Tanner guessed the cousins received more money under the table in the form of cash being funneled through the black ops program.

He was thinking of waiting for them to return to their apartment so he could talk to them, then decided to let that go for now. Why, he didn't know, but his gut was telling him to be patient. It wasn't easy. He wanted nothing more than to get a name out of them that would lead him to whomever had killed Tonya.

He felt sick whenever he thought of her, and the tragedy of her life ending so young. He missed her, ached for her actually, although he was still certain he hadn't loved her. Maybe love would have grown in time. If so, Tonya's killer had robbed him of that.

Tanner left the apartment as he had found it and went back to where Kevin had parked his Honda. He'd wait to see if the men were spending the night or not. It wasn't yet ten o'clock. If they left, they might go somewhere else, rather than returning home.

The cousins left the apartment building at eight minutes after ten. Both men were smiling, having just gotten laid. Tanner wasn't smiling. His woman was dead.

When Kevin drove straight, instead of hanging a U-turn to head toward his apartment, Tanner was glad he had stuck with the men.

They wound up on a street in East New York, Brooklyn. There were prostitutes climbing in and out of cars and doing a good business. Tanner wondered what Kevin and Kelly were doing there. Maybe they hadn't had sex with the women after all, or they wanted more. The two ignored the women and drove another block to park behind a van with a wild paint job. A similar van was parked nearby.

Men stepped out of vans. One was black and the other

was white. Both men were huge and had obviously lifted a lot of weights in their time. They met Kevin and Kelly as they left their car. Tanner had parked on the opposite side of the street and was half a block away. After removing a pair of binoculars from the glove box, he adjusted the focus to see what was going on.

It appeared the men from the vans and the cousins knew each other, as they greeted one another while bumping fists. It was possible they had all served time together.

They spoke for a minute before the white man walked over and opened the rear of the van. Tanner could make out the corner of a mattress. When the man motioned to someone inside the van, a girl emerged.

She was white, skinny, maybe as old as fifteen. She was wearing makeup and had on a red string bikini. There was little for the bikini top to cover. Tanner felt his grip on the binoculars tighten as bile rose in his throat. The girl was being pimped out. He looked at the other van and wondered if there was another underage girl inside that one. There was. It was another young white girl who was maybe a year or two younger than the other one, and no taller than five feet high. She was dressed like the first girl. Sometimes it was hell you could thank for little girls, and not heaven, as an old song once said.

Kevin and Kelly chose the younger of the two children and passed an envelope to the white pimp after looking the girl over. The envelope was thick. Tanner assumed there was money in it. When the meeting ended, the girls climbed back inside their vans and the cousins took off. Tanner followed them reluctantly. He had to fight the urge to drive over and shoot the black and white child pimps to death.

He would have done so, but the time wasn't right, and he'd be risking the girls getting caught in a firefight.

A phone call to the police might get the men arrested, but the police would have to be blind not to know that there was prostitution going on in the area. The legal system used prostitutes as a revenue source. They would round them up every once in a while, fine them, then release them, only to do it all again. With the child pimps being so blatant about how they went about their business, it was a safe bet that they would receive a warning from a corrupt cop if they were in danger of being busted. And if they were busted, they would be back on the street someday soon with different girls. No. Tanner would handle them his way, with a permanent solution.

Kevin and Kelly drove to their apartment. Tanner watched the lights come on only to go out twenty minutes later. It looked like the cousins were in for the night.

Tanner returned to his hotel for a few hours of sleep. In the morning, he would resume watching the cousins. They were up to something. Since it was their job to set up people to take a fall, whatever they were doing would likely ruin someone's life.

Tanner sighed as he turned off the light in his room after showering. It was unlikely either man had been driving the car that killed Tonya. That didn't mean they wouldn't know who had. He would make them talk after he figured out what they were up to.

9

NEW EVIDENCE

Detective Blum worked the midday shift. That was why she had time to accompany Thaxton to Yonkers in the morning to speak with Michael Hallam's widow, Eve.

Eve Hallam was a hefty woman in her fifties who worked as a real estate agent. Her eyes were red from crying over the loss of her husband. They had been separated, but she had still loved him.

Thaxton started the conversation by telling Eve how sorry he was for her loss. She thanked him and asked them why they were there.

Blum explained that although her husband's death was an open case, the hit-and-run allegations had been settled and Tonya Wilson's death had officially been lain on her husband's doorstep.

Eve Hallam shook her head. "Michael didn't do that."

Thaxton studied her. "Why do you say that with such conviction?"

"Michael was a drunk, he cheated on me, and I didn't want to share my life with him any longer, but the man was not a liar. We were married for over thirty years, and I knew everything about him. When I asked him if he had run that woman over, he swore he hadn't left the house. He'd been drinking, yes, but he remembered every moment of that night."

"He was certain he hadn't blacked out and forgotten the whole incident?" Blum asked.

"He never suffered from blackouts, he just couldn't stop drinking, and nothing helped. I might have stayed with him if it had just been that, but I couldn't abide his unfaithfulness."

"Who did he have an affair with?" Thaxton asked.

Eve's face formed into a scowl. "That he wouldn't say. He told me the next day he had slept with her, but he said I didn't need to know who she was. I did see her once. She was getting in her car as I was pulling into the driveway. She was a skinny bitch, but I never got a good look at her face."

"Why did he confess the affair to you?" Blum asked.

"He said he couldn't live with the guilt. That was Michael. If he had killed that woman… are you certain he didn't kill himself?"

"I am," Blum said. "And so are the Yonkers detectives handling the case. There is no way your husband could have clasped his hands together in the manner he was found. The killer also shot him in the right temple, although your husband was left-handed."

"And you think the woman he had the affair with might have killed him?"

Blum held up a hand. "I didn't say that. I'm also not working that case."

"Michael said she was angry with him. That was why she came to see him. She slept with him so he would help her with a problem."

"What was that problem?" Thaxton asked.

"Michael never said. He claimed he was drunk when they slept together and that he was too stupid to see she was just using him for his influence."

"His influence? Was he still employed at Dangal Corp. when the affair happened?"

"Yes. It was a few days later that he was fired, after losing his license for driving drunk again."

Thaxton and Blum shared a look. If the woman had wanted Hallam to use his influence at Dangal Corp. to help her, it was likely she worked there.

"Mrs. Hallam," Blum said. "Are you aware of what Tonya Wilson looked like?"

"I saw a photo of her in the paper. She was beautiful."

"Could she have been the woman your husband had the affair with?"

The question startled Eve. She looked thoughtful. "I guess it's possible, but I never saw her face."

"Do you remember what she was wearing?" Thaxton asked.

"I do. It was a green top with long sleeves, or it might have been a dress. She was halfway inside the car when I spotted her."

"And what kind of car was it?"

"That I couldn't tell you. Cars all look alike to me. It wasn't very big or a sports car, I can say that."

"And speaking of cars, may I get a look at the car that was involved in the hit-and-run accident?"

"It's in the garage. It was towed here after Michael paid the impound lot. I don't know what to do with it. I certainly don't ever want to drive it again, and it suffered damage. I'll likely end up selling it as is."

Eve used a key to unlock a side door of the detached garage. The Caddy was there with its missing side-view mirror. Considering the vehicle had struck a grown woman, its front end had suffered little damage.

Thaxton opened it up and looked through it. There was half a crushed cigarette in the ashtray. He looked at Eve.

"Did your husband smoke cigarettes?"

"Yes, but usually only when he was drinking or felt stressed."

After finding something on the floor, Thaxton pointed out the object. It was a tube of lip balm that was on a floor mat between the pedals. There was grit from the floor covering the tip of the strawberry flavored balm.

"Do you recognize that, Mrs. Hallam?"

Eve leaned into the car and studied the object. "It's not mine. And Michael never used lip balm."

"Please don't touch it," Blum said. "It could be evidence that someone other than your husband was driving the car. I'll call the Yonkers Police and let them know it's there."

Eve looked confused. "I thought you were handling the hit-and-run case."

"I was. It's possible that whoever killed your husband also tried to frame him for that murder."

"The woman he slept with?"

"It's possible, or maybe someone she's involved with became jealous. Your young neighbor claimed to see a man with your husband yesterday, shortly before his death."

Eve began crying. "Oh, how I wish Michael had been a stronger man. I thought the alcohol would kill him someday, not involvement in some tawdry love triangle."

Thaxton ran a hand over the dent in the Caddy's hood. Someone other than Michael Hallam had killed Tonya Wilson. He was determined to find them.

10

RESCUE AT SEA

Tanner followed Kevin and Kelly the next morning after setting up outside their apartment building at five-thirty. The cousins didn't come out until seven a.m., then they headed to a coffee shop near the Lincoln Tunnel. They took a cab instead of the car.

The white pimp was there, along with the girl Tanner had seen the night before. She was wearing a dress and had ribbons in her hair. The girl never spoke as far as Tanner could see. She had probably been trained not to speak or was too traumatized to do so.

The men ate, and the girl consumed a plate of eggs. She didn't appear to enjoy it. When Kevin and Kelly left the coffee shop, the girl went with them.

Tanner had parked in a spot where the meter was broken. He came out to find a ticket on his windshield. He tossed it into the back seat and started the car. The cousins had flagged down a taxi and were headed toward the tunnel entrance. Tanner was glad to see the cab drive past it. If they had taken the tunnel, he could have been in for a long trip.

It turned out to be a short trip that ended at Chelsea Piers. That might mean the cousins were getting on a boat. If they were, they were having trouble locating it, as Tanner watched them wander around the pier.

They located the boat they wanted nine minutes later. It was a white cabin cruiser named *The Molly Sue*. Kelly kept watch while Kevin went aboard. The girl stayed with Kelly and kept her head down. Kevin signaled his cousin after gaining entry to the cabin, and the men went below with the girl.

"What the hell are they doing?" Tanner said to himself and wondered if they were hurting the girl. They returned to the deck without her a minute later. Before shutting the door to the cabin, Kelly had called down to the girl. Tanner released a long breath. It appeared the girl was all right.

The men left the boat and strolled along the dock until they were back near the buildings that faced the piers. Tanner noticed they kept checking their watches. When a man arrived wearing white slacks and a white shirt, the cousins high-fived each other. That same man boarded the boat they had been on. He was about fifty, looked to be in good shape, and had graying hair.

Tanner saw signs that he was planning to take the boat out and decided to follow him.

"Where is it you want to go?"

The question came from a man with a charter boat. He'd been set to take a group out for the afternoon, but they had called and asked to reschedule. Their car had crapped out on them on the Connecticut Turnpike, then one of their kids had thrown up and displayed signs of having a fever.

"I just want to go out on the water for an hour or two," Tanner said. "How much will that cost?"

The man thought about it and answered in a tentative voice. "Um, one-fifty an hour? That includes beer and snacks."

"Sold. When can we get underway?"

"I'm ready to go now."

Tanner looked at the cabin cruiser the girl was on. "Let's get going."

THE OWNER OF THE CHARTER BOAT WAS NAMED DAVE. Tanner told Dave his name was Steve and gave him three hundred dollars. Tanner had kept them close to the cabin cruiser without actually saying, "Follow that boat," but when it was the only vessel nearby, Dave noticed.

"Hey, um, your wife isn't on that boat with another guy, is she?"

Tanner smiled. "It's nothing like that; I guess we're just going the same way they are."

Dave covered his eyes with his hand to block out glare and frowned. "You know, I think that boat is taking on water. She seems to be sitting awfully low."

"Get closer. There's something wrong."

Dave had been right; the cabin cruiser was sinking, as Kevin and Kelly had intended. The owner of the boat was waving them down, although they were obviously headed toward him. He was standing on the deck with the girl beside him. The dress was gone, and she was wearing only the string bikini Tanner had seen her in the night before.

Dave noticed. "What the hell? Why is that little girl dressed like that?"

"We'll figure that out after we rescue them; that boat is sinking fast."

The owner of the cabin cruiser was Joseph Cook. He was the vice president of a corporation that was a rival to Dangal Corp. The plan had been for Cook to be found on his boat with an underage girl. He would have not only lost his sterling reputation, but also his job, and possibly his freedom. He climbed aboard after helping Tanner with the girl and began explaining right away.

"I swear to God I don't know where this child came from or why she's dressed like this. She nearly scared me to death when she popped out from a storage space that's beneath a bench."

Dave pointed south. There was a vessel approaching. After raising binoculars, he said it looked like the coast guard. Joseph Cook's face turned white.

"I can't be caught with this girl. Oh God, I think someone is trying to set me up. Please. I'm begging. Get me out of here."

"Get moving, Dave."

Dave was looking at Cook with suspicious eyes. Tanner leaned in and spoke to him so only he could hear.

"Remember you suspected I was following this boat? I was. The man is right. He was set up. I'm here to help him."

Dave spoke in an equally low voice. "He's telling the truth?"

"Yeah."

"Okay. I'll help him. But we'd better hurry."

Dave headed back toward the pier. He was closing in on it when the coast guard made contact with him over the radio. He told them that yes, he had rescued the lone man on board. They would be waiting for them along Pier 59.

When he was done, Dave asked Tanner about the girl.

"Call the police and explain that you found her wandering along the pier."

"What if she says different?"

"I don't think she's in a talking mood," Tanner said. He leaned over and spoke to the girl. She wouldn't meet his eyes but continued to look down. "You don't have to worry about the men who hurt you ever again."

The child lifted her head and her eyes flicked left to meet Tanner's intense gaze. A small smile played on her lips as she looked away. She had glimpsed the truth in Tanner's eyes. The pimps who had abused her would soon never hurt anyone else again.

Tanner ignored Dave's calls for him to stay and help and headed away from the boat. He was looking for Kevin and Kelly. They weren't there. After calling the coast guard and telling them about a sinking boat that was southeast of the piers. They had been so confident about the outcome that they hadn't bothered to stick around.

He drove to their apartment house. Their car wasn't there. It also wasn't near the building where the women he had seen them with the night before lived. The same was true of Bloke's Bar. He returned to their apartment, picked the lock again, and waited for them.

After getting an idea, he left for an hour, did some shopping, then returned to the apartment house but didn't go inside. The cousins came home at nine-thirty. They were talking loud as if they had been drinking. Tanner stole their car while wearing gloves. He had need of it.

65

TWENTY MINUTES LATER, HE WAS IN EAST NEW YORK, Brooklyn. The pimps with the vans were there, as was a customer, a fat man with long hair and a goatee. Tanner drove up as the fat man was stepping out of the rear of a van. It made his blood boil to think of what the son of a bitch had been doing in there.

The black pimp looked at him and had no reaction. Tanner was wearing a red wig. The guy had mistaken him for either Kevin or Kelly since he was driving their car. Tanner lowered his window and shot the black man twice in the chest, then sent two rounds into the belly of the fat man.

The white pimp had been inside his own van, behind the wheel. He leapt out holding a gun and took a bullet to the face. That shot had come from a different gun, one belonging to Kevin Doyle. The first shots had come from a weapon that had Kelly's fingerprints on it.

There were a few people near enough to see what had happened. They were mostly hookers. If they talked to the police, which was doubtful, they would report having seen a man with red hair doing the shooting.

The pimps weren't making a sound, but the fat customer was releasing howls of agony from his gut wounds. Tanner thought the sick bastard couldn't suffer enough. He drove away at a normal speed and was headed back to leave the car in front of Kevin and Kelly's apartment house. It had done what he hoped it would do. It made the pimps think he was Kevin or Kelly come to call. They had never gotten off a shot, which might have placed the girl inside the van in danger.

Knowing the cops, it would take them a while to tie the cousins to the murders.

That was okay. Tanner would use that time to find out more information. He passed a speeding police car headed the other way and thought about the girl who was in the rear of the van. She would get help, but she might never recover from the trauma she'd been through.

She was alive, though. Some girls didn't survive to grow into women. That had been true of Tanner's own sisters, Jesse and Jill.

Tanner left the car where it had been parked when he'd taken it. The two guns were hidden in the trunk, and the wig he'd been wearing was shoved down a sewer.

Tanner went back to his hotel to grab a few hours of sleep. When he dreamt, he dreamt of Tonya.

11

FOLLOW THAT CAR

THAXTON WAS IN A JUICE BAR IN QUEENS TALKING TO A woman who was young enough to be his daughter. He wasn't out on a date; he was meeting with a source.

Holly Tepper had strawberry blonde hair and the tattoo of a red rose on the back of her right hand. She was a competitive marathon runner and the healthiest person Thaxton had ever known. The woman literally glowed with vitality. It had been her idea to meet in the juice bar. She was always trying to convert people to her way of thinking. Thaxton had agreed. It wouldn't hurt him to eat healthier.

The juice bar occupied a small storefront and only had a few tables. There were nine other people in the store. Thaxton was certain he was a good twenty years older than all of them.

Holly had chosen his drink for him. It was some sort of concoction made from several vegetables. Thaxton had taken his first sip with caution, then found that he liked the drink. It tasted like tomato juice… mostly. It reminded him of a Bloody Mary without the vodka.

Holly grinned at him with her straight white teeth. "It's good, right?"

"It is good. Thanks for suggesting it."

"You're welcome. I guess you want to know if I have any news, hmm?"

"Do you?"

"Not much. Some executive was fired recently for his problem with alcoholism. I heard he ran a woman down the other day, and today I heard he was dead."

"I know about that. His name was Michael Hallam."

"Oh. Um, there are two new employees who have criminal records."

"Really? What were their offenses?"

"Armed robbery. The two spent ten years in prison. Can you imagine being locked up like that? I'd go nuts if I couldn't run every day."

"Do you know their names?"

Holly had a small pink purse with her. She removed a slip of paper from it. It contained Kevin and Kelly's names and their address.

"This could lead to something, thank you," Thaxton said, and passed Holly an envelope. It contained two hundred dollars.

Holly slid the envelope into her purse without looking inside it.

"I have something else."

"What's that?"

"Kevin and Kelly aren't the only criminal types that are working at Dangal Corp. They're just the only ones doing so officially. Some really rough-looking men have been seen in the building. They have key cards, but none of them are listed as being employed with the corporation. My supervisor told everyone to ignore it. She said the men were with security. But that doesn't make sense, and they're never in the building for very long."

"How many men are we talking about?"

"I've seen three different guys; they are usually together."

"Describe them."

"Hairy is the best way to describe them. They all have long hair and beards."

"They sound like bikers."

Holly was nodding at that suggestion. "Yeah. You know, you're right. They remind me of bikers. Only I've never seen them wearing leather vests or anything."

"Do you have any names for them?"

"No, sorry."

"Don't be. You've given me a place to start."

"Something really shady is going on, hmm?"

"I think so. Stay away from that Kevin and Kelly and the others."

"Kevin tried hitting on me. The dude's like forty. My dad is only forty-two. Oh, did I mention they both have red hair?"

"You have now."

"They look alike, but they're cousins instead of brothers."

"I'll follow them and see what they get up to."

"I saw them entering the building as I was leaving. They might still be there."

"Then I should get going," Thaxton said as he stood. He placed a ten on the table. "Have another juice drink on me."

Holly grinned. "Thanks, Richard."

A minute later, Thaxton was in his car and headed toward the headquarters of Dangal Corp.

~

KEVIN AND KELLY WERE STILL INSIDE THE BUILDING. THEY had been called in after hours to have a meeting with Brent Hayward. Hayward was a graduate of Princeton and had grown up in the town. He had been employed by the Dangal Corp. since leaving college twenty years earlier and had the ambition of someday running the corporation. The black ops division was his idea, but it had initially been handed over to someone else to run. That man had lacked imagination. Now that he had control of it, the black ops division was running the way it should have been all along.

Dangal Corp. had gained an additional nineteen percent of market share in their field since he'd taken control of the black ops division. That growth came about by causing havoc to their competitors through manipulation, theft of corporate secrets, and bringing misfortune to the key employees of their rivals. Murder had also been used on occasion. That was something that Brent Hayward kept mainly to himself. One exception was his right-hand man, James Archer. If the authorities ever became involved, Hayward planned to use Archer as a sacrificial lamb.

Kevin and Kelly had been given the task of discrediting Joseph Cook, the vice president of development at a rival corporation. They would have succeeded in doing so had Tanner not interfered the day before by rescuing Cook and the girl who had been hidden away on his boat. Had the coast guard rescued Cook instead of Tanner, there would have been an official record of Cook having been with the child prostitute. Cook's career would have ended no matter how vociferously he might have proclaimed his innocence. His reputation and marriage would have also been damaged irrevocably.

Brent Hayward didn't care about that. His only concern had been to remove Cook from his position, so the corporation he worked for would be weakened. Kevin and Kelly had failed; Hayward wanted to know why.

Kelly shrugged. "We don't know what happened. The coast guard should have found the girl on Cook's boat when they rescued him. Shit. Do you think he drowned the girl so she wouldn't be found?"

"He didn't drown the girl, you idiot. Someone else rescued him before the coast guard reached him. That girl you used was handed over to child services."

"We sabotaged the boat, then called the coast guard and told them about the boat sinking as soon as Cook left the pier. It was just bad luck that someone reached him before they did," Kevin said.

"That bad luck cost the corporation thousands of dollars and Cook still needs to be removed from his position. The man is too good at his job."

"We could try something else," Kelly said. "Maybe set him up with an underaged male hooker. That would get him canned."

Hayward considered it while running an index finger across his mustache. He then shook his head.

"We'll leave him be for now and move on to a different target. And you two get out of here. I'm sick of looking at you."

KEVIN WAS COMPLAINING TO HIS COUSIN AS HE UNLOCKED his car and climbed inside.

"How many setups have we done? Over a dozen, right? And there were no problems. One thing goes wrong, and Hayward gives us shit."

"Screw him. He'll get over it. Right now, I want to go back to Bloke's Bar and see if those girls are there again tonight."

"Hell yeah. Maybe we can talk them into switching off this time. My girl was hot, but the one you had was cute too."

"You think they'll go for that?"

Kevin laughed. "Maybe, if we get them drunk enough." He expected to hear Kelly laugh along, but his cousin was silent. When Kevin turned his head to look at him, he saw the reason for Kelly's silence.

Tanner was in the back seat of the car. There was a gun in his hand, and its tip was pressed against the back of Kelly's head.

"Start your engine and I'll tell you where to drive to."

"Are you carjacking us?"

"No. This is something different. I want information. You two are going to give it to me."

"Do as he says, Kevin, or the dude might blow my brains out."

Kevin started the engine and Tanner told him to drive straight for several blocks. Kevin looked at him by using the rearview mirror.

"Who are you?"

"I'm the man with a gun who will kill you both if you don't do everything I say. That's who I am."

Kevin remained quiet after that. He never noticed the black car pulling away from the curb behind them.

That car was being driven by Thaxton. He had just arrived in the area when he saw Tanner pop up in the back seat of Kevin's car and place a gun to Kelly's head.

He too wanted answers, so he was following Kevin, while wondering who Tanner was, and what he intended to do to the cousins.

Thaxton followed as Kevin drove uptown. Holly's tip was definitely paying off.

12

TRUE CONFESSIONS

TANNER HAD INSTRUCTED KEVIN TO DRIVE TO HARLEM. They wound up at the rear of an old factory that hadn't been in production in more than twenty years. The place used to make tire rims. Back in the 1940s, it produced helmets for the war effort.

These days, it granted shelter to a homeless man who was out scavenging through local dumpsters. Tanner instructed Kevin and Kelly to enter the building through the gap where a side door had once been. The men looked nervous. They had a right to be.

After patting them down for weapons and finding two folding knives, Tanner made them sit on the floor.

Kelly pointed at him. "You were in the bar the other night."

"And now I'm here. What do you two know about Tonya Wilson's death?"

"Who?" Kevin said.

"She was the chick that got run over," Kelly told his cousin. "Michael Hallam did that, then he committed suicide. At least, that's what we heard."

"Hallam didn't kill Tonya. Someone else did. I'm wondering if it was one of you two."

The cousins were shaking their heads, then Kevin spoke.

"We've never killed anybody."

"What about the other men Hayward has working for him?"

"Those guys are muscle he hired to start trouble inside a union. If the union goes on strike, one of Dangal Corp's competitors will be screwed."

"And the bikers, Lucifer's Angels? What's their job?"

"Is that story true?" Kelly said. "We've only heard rumors about that."

"I was told that executives from other companies have been having fatal accidents. Tonya had a fatal accident too."

"We only heard about one, but he worked for Dangal Corp. The guy wanted to end the black ops program. That same executive died during a business trip to California. They say he was killed by a homeless man who had a long beard. Most bikers have long beards."

"And what else do you know about the murders?"

"Nothing," Kevin said. "I swear to God. We were thieves before taking this job, and even now we never really hurt anyone... not physically."

"You just go around ruining people's lives? Is that what you mean?"

The cousins looked away. They were both startled when something slapped against the floor between them.

Tanner had thrown down a pair of small blue notebooks that had pens stuck in their spiraled wire bindings.

"I want you two to write down everything you've done for Dangal Corp. That includes the names of your victims and the dates when it happened. If you try to scribble out a lie, your stories won't agree with each other. If that happens, I'll be forced to shoot you, since you'll be no use to me."

The cousins gave each other stricken looks. Kelly asked a question.

"Are you a cop?"

"I'm like you. I work for a corporation. We've caught on to what Hayward is doing. Now, we're fighting fire with fire. Once I have your confessions written down, and signed, I can hold them over your heads. You two are going to be my spies inside Dangal Corp. Start writing."

Kevin shook his head. "I won't do it. If the cops ever found what I wrote down they would put me back in prison for another ten years, hell, maybe more than that."

Tanner aimed his gun at him. "Write or die. Those are your choices. I'll give you ten seconds to decide."

It hadn't taken Kevin ten seconds to decide. It took one look into Tanner's eyes to know that he was telling the truth. If he refused to do as he was told, he and his cousin would die inside the old factory.

Both men began writing. At one point, Kelly became stumped by something and asked his cousin a question.

"I don't want you talking to each other."

"But I can't remember the name of the guy we framed for drug possession a few months back. It was a weird name and started with a C and had the word win in it. Something like Comwinky, Caswinski…"

"It was Czerwinski," Kevin said. "Melvin Czerwinski. Remember how hot his daughter was?"

"Oh, hell yeah. The girl was only eighteen, and she had four boyfriends. One of them was the guy who cut the grass and—"

"That's enough talking. Keep writing. And sign them

when you're done. I also want a phone number I can reach you at. From now on, you work for me, not Brent Hayward."

Kevin raised his hand as if he were still in grade school. "Do we have to write down what we did yesterday?"

"Yes."

"But it didn't work, and you already know about it."

"Write it down anyway, but don't mention Joseph Cook's name."

～

THAXTON HAD STAYED WITH HIS CAR AND WAITED TO SEE what would happen. There weren't many places to hide. If someone left the building, they would spot him walking toward it. After several minutes passed, he grew too curious to stay put and crept toward the building. He had feared he might hear a pair of gunshots signaling Kevin and Kelly's deaths, but it had been quiet. The factory was a good place to bring someone if you planned to murder them.

By the time he reached a window to look through, he saw Kevin and Kelly rising from the floor. They were handing something to the man, who was still holding a gun on them. They were small notebooks. The man with the gun read through them quickly, then he said something to the cousins, but Thaxton wasn't able to make out what it was.

～

"WE CAN REALLY GO?" KEVIN ASKED.

"That's right. I'll be in touch soon. If Hayward gives you another assignment, I want to hear about it."

"What should we call you?"

"Boss will work. Let's leave here. I have other things to do."

THAXTON WATCHED THE MEN GO. HE HAD GOTTEN A GOOD look at Tanner and wondered if he had been Tonya Wilson's boyfriend, the one who had been described as having serious eyes.

He waited until he heard Kevin's car start up and drive away before he headed back to his own car. He was ten feet from the building when a voice spoke to him from behind.

"Turn around slowly while keeping your hands in sight."

Thaxton cursed himself for having jumped to the conclusion that all three men had driven away. He raised his empty hands to shoulder level and turned around. Tanner was staring at him. He held a gun but it was pointed at the ground.

"Who are you?"

"I'm a private investigator named Richard Thaxton. I take it your name is Tanner?"

"Toss me your ID. There's a weapon on your right hip. It would be a bad idea for you to reach for it."

"I understand. My wallet is in my back pocket. I'll take it out slowly."

The wallet was tossed over. Tanner caught it before it could hit the ground. He opened it to see Thaxton's private investigator's license. There was also a photo of a smiling woman standing beside a younger version of Thaxton. That woman was Detective Blum.

Tanner tossed him back the wallet and put his gun away.

"Who are you working for, Thaxton?"

"My client's wife was murdered months ago, along with her assistant. Someone tried to make it look as if they had been having an affair. I intend to find the murderer and clear the wife's name and restore her reputation."

"She'll still be dead."

"Yeah, but her husband is alive, and he can't stand to have people think the worst of her."

"Why were you following Kevin and Kelly?"

"I was told they might be up to no good."

"You were told right," Tanner said. He handed Thaxton the notebooks with the cousins' confessions in them. Thaxton took them and noticed that Tanner was wearing a pair of clear gloves.

"What are these?"

"Inside is a list of the 'no good' Kevin and Kelly have been up to over the last few months. Your client's name isn't in there. They're scumbags, but they don't deal in violence."

Thaxton read the first page of Kevin's notebook, then flipped through it and read some more. He wore a look of disgust as he handed the notebooks back.

"The shit they've done. Why the hell did they write it all down?"

"I said I would kill them if they didn't."

"And would you have?"

"Let's go somewhere and talk. I think we're after the same thing, more or less."

"You want to know who killed your girl, Tonya Wilson?"

"That's right."

"Someone told me that Dangal Corp. may have bikers

working for them. If anyone is involved in murder, my guess would be that they're the ones handling it."

Thaxton told Tanner he had left his car in front, parked across the street from the entrance to the factory's parking lot. They walked to it in silence, but Thaxton asked Tanner a question before getting in the car.

"Did you kill Michael Hallam?"

"No."

"He was murdered. He had an affair with someone shortly before he was fired from Dangal Corp. It could be the woman's boyfriend or husband who was out for revenge."

"Do you have the woman's name?"

"No, but a neighbor saw Hallam talking to a thin man wearing a yellow hoodie on the morning of the day he was killed. Does that sound familiar?"

"Whoever drove the car that killed Tonya was wearing a yellow hoodie. I never saw their face."

"Hey Tanner, I'm sorry about what happened to your girl."

"Not as sorry as the person who killed her will be."

Thaxton understood what Tanner meant. He planned to kill Tonya's murderer. That was fine by him. If anyone had run down Colleen Blum the way Tonya had been, he knew he wouldn't rest until he had killed them.

They got inside the car and Thaxton suggested they find a bar to talk in.

"We'll go to one that serves food. All I've had since breakfast was a glass of tomato juice."

Thaxton drove south out of Harlem, with his brooding passenger beside him.

13

BUSTED

Tanner found himself liking Thaxton. The man was a straight shooter. When they were settled in a booth together inside a bar, he told Tanner he would go first and proceeded to tell him everything he had learned from Blum about the investigation into Tonya's death.

It surprised Tanner that Blum had enlisted Thaxton to help find out the truth, although the police department had ruled Tonya's death an accident.

"This detective, Blum, she must trust you to come to you for help."

"We've known each other for a lot of years. She may have been pulled off your girl's case, it doesn't mean she's willing to let a killer go free."

They had both ordered cheeseburgers and were drinking beer. The food came over and was delivered by a young, blonde waitress. She smiled at Tanner and asked him to be sure to tell her if there was anything else he needed.

"I think someone likes you," Thaxton said, as the waitress walked away.

"Someone who won't like me is Brent Hayward. I was told by two people that he's the man running Dangal's black ops division. I plan to follow him when I leave here."

Thaxton raised his eyebrows. "Black ops division? Is that what they're calling it?"

"Yeah."

"Did you know your girl was a part of that?"

"She never had the chance to tell me, but yeah, she was working as a corporate spy."

"Maybe she was killed because she had found out something she shouldn't have. Did she seem nervous the last time you spoke?"

"She wasn't nervous. Tonya was thinking of quitting her job. She didn't like what had been going on there lately."

"While you're following Hayward around, I'm going to see what I can learn about this biker gang you told me about, Lucifer's Angels. And um, what do you plan to do with those confessions you have?"

"Kevin and Kelly think I'm using them, so they'll spy on Hayward for me."

"Aren't you doing that?"

"No. I have other plans for those two. They crossed the line when they tried using an underage girl in one of their schemes yesterday."

"I guess you're not planning on killing them or they would already be dead."

"Guys like that will suffer more in prison. Although I was tempted to shoot them."

"If they wanted to stay out of prison, they should have gone straight after getting out, instead of hooking up with a piece of work like Hayward."

∼

KEVIN AND KELLY HAD DRIVEN BACK TO DANGAL CORP. after leaving Tanner. They figured Brent Hayward might be able to help them. They told Hayward about their encounter with Tanner and that he was asking questions about Tonya's death. They thought it would be better to say something rather than attempt to hide it. However, they left out the part about writing down their confessions.

Hayward's assistant, James Archer, was present. Archer was thirty-six, thin, and still looked like a preppy college kid, despite the suit he was wearing. His tie was yellow and matched his socks.

Hayward told Kevin and Kelly to wait in the outer office while he spoke to Archer. When they had shut the door behind them, Hayward asked Archer what he thought about their story.

"It sounds like someone from another company is coming after us. I didn't like hearing about the gun. It means the man might be a serious threat."

"I'm not sure I agree. Why would a rival spy from another company be concerned about what had happened to Tonya? No, I think this may be something more personal, unless his story about knowing Tonya was an act. Contact Steelman. We'll need his people to handle this."

Steelman was the name of the man who was in charge of Lucifer's Angels. Hayward was paying the biker gang to commit murders.

"How can the motorcycle gang handle it? We have no idea who we're dealing with."

"Whoever it is will come after me, eventually. Tell Steelman I want to set up a trap... a fatal trap."

"That will cost more money, and we're nearing our budget for this quarter."

"It will be fine. After how much we've helped to increase business, our operating budget has been doubled.

I also managed to acquire bonuses. Yours will be twenty thousand dollars."

Archer grinned. "Excellent. What about Kevin and Kelly? What should I tell them?"

Hayward considered the cousins. They had come directly to him after being accosted. That counted for something.

"Tell them to get out of the city for a while and that we'll contact them when we want them to return."

"Any suggestions about where they should go?"

"Give them two hundred each from petty cash to gamble with and send them to Atlantic City. That will be close enough so we can get them back here in a few hours if we need them."

"You're willing to give them money after their failure yesterday?"

Hayward smiled. "I received a two-thousand-dollar bonus for each of them. I'll be keeping that for myself."

"Ah, I see."

"And call Steelman as soon as you can."

"Yes, sir."

KEVIN AND KELLY LEFT THE BUILDING FIFTEEN MINUTES later. They were still worried about Tanner, but they were sure Hayward would know how to handle him. They only hoped Tanner died before he could use their confessions against them.

They were going to ignore the suggestion that they stay in Atlantic City and head up to Boston to crash with a friend they knew. If those confessions fell into the wrong hands, they did not want to be easy to find.

They were so preoccupied with their problems that

neither of them noticed the unmarked police car parked behind them. When a plainclothes cop and his partner stepped out and identified themselves while reaching for guns, they figured Tanner had screwed them. He had, but not in the way they believed.

"Murder?" Kevin said.

The cop nodded as his partner placed handcuffs on Kelly.

"That's right. Two counts of murder and one count of attempted murder. Or maybe it's three counts of murder by now. The fat guy in the ICU could have cashed in his chips; he was in bad shape when we saw him."

"Who are we supposed to have killed?" Kelly asked.

"A pair of pimps who specialize in underage girls. And oh, yeah, one of their customers."

"Rico and Tony are dead?" Kevin said.

"That's them," the cop said.

A squad car pulled up with its lights flashing and its engine off.

When they searched Kevin's car after placing Kevin in the squad car and Kelly in the unmarked vehicle, they found the guns Tanner had used to kill the pimps.

"We'll have to run these through ballistics," the cop told his partner, "but I'll bet you a dinner that they'll match the slugs taken from the bodies."

"No bet," said the partner. "Anyway, just having weapons will keep these two in jail for a while, not to mention the knives they were carrying."

Kevin stared out the window of the squad car he was in and saw the stunned look he had on his face being mirrored by his cousin. They were both royally screwed, and they knew it.

When the police entered Dangal Corp. to enquire about the cousins, they were told that they had been given menial jobs to do as part of a government program to help ex-cons get on their feet. It was a shame that the Doyle cousins weren't worthy of getting a second chance.

When Brent Hayward was informed of their arrest, he had Archer phony up records showing that Kevin and Kelly had been written up for breaking the rules several times over the last few weeks, along with a company document stating they had been fired two days earlier for suspected theft of company property. It was the same tactic he had used to get rid of Rae Houghton weeks earlier.

1 4

LABOR AT A HIGHER LEVEL

STEELMAN WAS THE ACTUAL SURNAME OF THE MAN WHO had founded the motorcycle club Lucifer's Angels. He never told anyone that his first name was Albert.

Steelman was thirty-four and had nineteen men in his club, which he had started after leaving a Hell's Angels chapter out in California a dozen years ago.

His club was based in New Jersey, where he had grown up and where he returned when he learned that his mother was dying of cancer. His mother had been the only person he'd ever loved. He cried when she died, then went on a three-day binge of drunkenness, rape, and pillaging that had left four drug dealers dead, a drug dealer's girlfriend ravaged, then later killed, and Steelman was two-hundred thousand richer.

Not all of his ill-gotten gain had been cash. Most of that two-hundred thousand had been in the form of crack cocaine.

When Brent Hayward was looking around for someone to commit murder when needed, he spoke to an employee he knew had a shady past. That person connected him with Steelman, by way of Archer, and the Lucifer's Angels motorcycle club had become the wet works team for Dangal's black ops program.

If anyone above Hayward had been aware he was sanctioning murders, he would have been dismissed. When a vice president of the corporation had attempted to rally others on Dangal's board to dismantle the black ops division, he found few who would agree with him. The program used dirty tactics. It was illegal as hell, could result in a huge fine, along with horrendous bad press if ever discovered by authorities. It had also created over sixty million in new profit since its inception.

Later, when rumors began to swirl about how convenient the accidental deaths of executives of rival companies had been, certain members of Dangal's board wondered if their black ops program had been behind them.

When asked about it in a session of the board that was held off the record, Brent Hayward denied knowing anything about it. He then went on the offensive and had Steelman murder his top opponent on the board. That was the man who had continually attempted to have the black ops division shut down. He was the one Kevin told Tanner had been killed by a homeless man.

After that incident, there was no further talk about ending the program, while Hayward had received praise and bonuses.

The consensus of the board members was that if Hayward had been behind the murders, at least he was on their side and making them money. They never spoke to each other about their fear that the man could become too powerful someday if he remained unchecked.

Hayward wanted that power. He had plans beyond someday controlling Dangal Corp. Why stop there? If he could wield the power of a legal corporation while also controlling a criminal organization, there was no telling how powerful he might become.

It was James Archer who contacted Steelman by phone to let him know what was going on, and about the threat Tanner represented.

Archer had grown up in Allentown, Pennsylvania, after the family had moved away from South Carolina when he was a baby. Why they settled there of all places, he never knew. His father had lacked ambition and spent his life as a laborer on construction sites for over twenty years. Many of the men he had worked with while young had gone on to learn a trade such as carpentry, plumbing, or even the skill of hanging wallboard. Not Archer's father. He did as little work as possible despite having three children to support.

Archer's mother worked when she could but was often ill from one ailment or another. Archer's older sisters moved away after marrying young and that left Archer alone with his parents. By then, his father was getting older, and he had trouble holding on to jobs that required a strong back. The man retired on a disability payment that placed them below the poverty line.

Archer pretended to be involved in after-school activities such as the chess club or the drama club. Instead, he made money tutoring other high school kids. He saved every dollar, left home at eighteen to move into a tiny apartment with a friend, and worked full time at a department store while putting himself through college.

He'd been smart enough to tutor kids who were less intelligent than him, but he was not at a level where he was going to be offered scholarships. He made it through college by attending at night with a degree in business and found work at Dangal Corp. Despite his degree, Archer had to settle for starting in the mailroom. He'd been told he'd be considered for a promotion upstairs when there was a vacancy, but two years later, he was still pushing a cart through the halls to deliver mail.

Brent Hayward had been a young executive at the time. He was hungry for advancement and not above using dirty tricks or underhandedness to aid his career. He had approached Archer one day and asked him to lunch, saying he had something he needed to discuss with him.

Hayward had made him an offer over lunch. Archer was to go through the mail of certain people in the company before delivering it and find anything of interest that could help Hayward. In return, Hayward would see to it that Archer advanced to a higher position that paid better.

Archer agreed to do it. He did not want to be a corporate version of his father and spend his life working in a lowly position. It was a thing of ease to look through the mail without anyone knowing. The interoffice envelopes weren't sealed in any meaningful way. A simple red string was looped around a tab to keep them closed.

Hayward used his advanced knowledge of decisions made by his superiors to make certain he was always on the right side of any issue that came up and was able to offer suggestions that made him seem more perceptive than he was.

Three months after enlisting Archer to be his spy within the company, Hayward received a substantial promotion and a generous bump in pay. After making certain he had someone else in the mailroom to aid him as Archer had done, Hayward promoted Archer to be his personal assistant. Nine years and several promotions later, Archer was Hayward's right-hand man and was making more in a month than he had in a year down in the mailroom. Much of that money was paid to him in the form of company stock or bonuses.

He'd been uneasy when Hayward had formed his alliance with Steelman and Lucifer's Angels. Steelman and the other bikers frightened him. The men were killers, murderers, and there didn't seem to be anything they wouldn't do if you paid them enough.

Steelman's gravelly voice came over the line when Archer phoned him to tell him about Tanner. He said that he would handle the problem.

"You have Hayward sit tight in that fancy office of his until you get a call from my men telling him they're in the city. They should be able to get there in a couple of hours."

"There will be heavy traffic at the tunnels and bridges this time of day," Archer reminded him.

Steelman laughed. "My boys will weave their hogs around the stupid four-wheelers. Rush hour don't bother us."

"You understand that Mr. Hayward wants this problem to be solved permanently, yes?"

"I get you. The guy will never bother you again, but we'll need Hayward's help to lead him into a trap."

"Will it involve risk?"

"Nah, he only has to ride around in that limo of his; my boys will do the rest."

"Thank you. You'll be paid the usual way."

"Hell yeah we will, or else."

"Um, yes. Goodbye."

The call ended, and Archer felt relief. Even talking to Steelman over the phone made him nervous. He called

Hayward and relayed to his boss what he'd been told by Steelman. Hayward said it was fine, because he had already planned to work late.

If his boss was working late, then so was Archer. He left his office to see what help he could be. He might be making more money than his father could have ever dreamed of earning, but he was still a laborer and a lackey who needed to stay in the good graces of his boss.

15

FOREVER

AFTER TALKING WITH THAXTON, TANNER ARRIVED AT Dangal Corp. in time to see Kevin's vehicle being loaded onto the rear of a tow truck from the police impound lot. He assumed that meant that the cops had linked the cousins to the killing of the two child pimps and their equally evil customer.

Tanner still had the notebooks with Kevin and Kelly's signed confessions in them. If he didn't need them as leverage when dealing with Hayward, he would later pass them on to Thaxton, who could make sure they wound up in the right hands. Whether they would be sentenced to prison for the murders of the pimps or made to pay for the chaos they had caused the innocent people they had framed for Hayward, Kevin and Kelly would be going back behind bars for a long time. Tanner only gave a damn about them because they had involved a child in one of their schemes. As he'd told Thaxton, that had crossed a line.

There was an underground garage beneath the

headquarters of Dangal Corp. that was reserved for company executives or important visitors to the building.

Tanner had learned about it from Thaxton, who had also told him that Hayward traveled around in a black limo. Tanner waited down the street from the garage's exit and kept watch for the vehicle. He didn't spot it until after eight at night.

The limousine headed away from Midtown and took the FDR Drive to the Brooklyn Bridge. Once they were in Brooklyn, the limo drove to a home on East 48th Street. The home was in a nice enough neighborhood but seemed modest. Tanner wondered if Hayward lived there or was visiting someone.

A visit seemed unlikely. The home was dark, as if no one were inside. Night had fallen while they had been traveling there. If there was anyone inside, they would have put on a lamp already.

Tanner had a description of Hayward. A man wearing a suit and matching his description appeared in a window after a light had come on. Hayward lowered the shades on the windows and another light came on in an upstairs window. Meanwhile, the limo driver had left, after having dropped off his passenger. It would seem that Hayward did live in the house. Yes. It would seem that way.

Tanner smiled while wondering if Hayward was tricky or if he was being paranoid by suspecting a trap. No, not paranoid, more like experienced in the ways of guile.

If Hayward knew Tanner had an interest in him, the man might set up a trap. Luring him inside a house would be one way to go about it.

Tanner had seen enough. He drove away. He would return and enter the home later, but there was no hurry. If Hayward was inside, the man would go to bed at some point, and Tanner could break in during the night to confront him. If a trap, then those waiting to spring it would grow weary during their wait.

Tanner returned to Manhattan, where he drove into an alley after spotting a large cardboard box. He used his knife to cut out the section of the box he wanted and placed it in the back seat of his car. After returning to his hotel, he went to bed early, intending to rise around three a.m.

If someone was back at that house in Brooklyn waiting for him, they were going to have a long and boring night.

TANNER ROSE SEVERAL MINUTES BEFORE HIS ALARM WAS TO go off and did an intense calisthenics workout before hitting the shower and shaving. He dressed in dark clothing and left the hotel before four a.m. After making a stop at a diner that was open all-night, he drove over the bridge and entered Brooklyn. Dawn was still more than an hour away and there was a light breeze blowing. The neighborhood was dark, but the main road nearby was busy with newspaper and bakery trucks making their deliveries, along with the vehicles of those who worked early shifts, such as nurses.

If anyone had been expecting Tanner to confront Hayward after having followed him to the house in Brooklyn, they certainly would have expected him to have made his move before now. Any level of alertness they had would have given way to boredom. Tanner was counting on that. He was also going to put an end to that state of boredom.

Two men were inside the house. They were members of the Lucifer's Angels Motorcycle Club and went by the names of Diesel and Scooter. Diesel was a beefy brute who stood six-foot-five. Scooter was nearly as tall but skinny. They had arrived in the city earlier, scouted out a home for sale, then removed the For Sale sign and broken in. A neighbor had noticed them and had walked over to ask the men what they were doing. Diesel had wrapped an arm around him, as if he were giving him a friendly hug. He had squeezed so hard that the neighbor had wheezed.

"What we're doing here is none of your damn business. If the cops show up, we're going to assume it was you who called them. Then, maybe soon, maybe not so soon, someone will come back here and burn your little house to the ground while you're asleep inside with your family. Do you understand what I'm saying to you?"

The neighbor had shaken his head wildly in response. When Diesel released him, the guy had run back inside his house and closed all the curtains.

Hayward had received a call from Diesel and Scooter, by way of Archer, instructing him to drive to the house in the limo and head around to the rear, where there was a garage. That was where Diesel and Scooter had stored their motorcycles. They would let Hayward inside the house through a rear door.

The house was empty of furniture, but there were white shades on all the windows. A pair of battery-powered lanterns could double as lamps. If anyone followed Hayward to the home, they would see him turn on the lights and lower the shades.

Hayward left in the limo afterward, and Diesel and Scooter settled in to wait.

By midnight, they had decided no one was coming and that they would take turns catching a few hours of sleep.

Scooter napped first. He was awake when the tapping at the rear door began. That door was off a back porch beyond the home's kitchen. Scooter peaked around the doorframe and saw the shadow of a figure at the door, beyond the drawn shade that covered the door's glass inset.

He moved into the living room and shook Diesel's shoulder to wake him. There was just enough light to see him in the gloom of the dark house. If not for the streetlights, the house would have been pitch black.

"We've got company. The guy is trying to pick the lock on the back door."

Diesel had been sitting on the floor in a corner of the living room with his back leaning up against the wall. He rose to his feet with startling speed, considering his size. That speed had shocked more than one of his opponents from rival gangs over the years, shortly before their deaths.

Scooter led the way to the rear door while taking out his knife. They planned to kill using blades. If they woke the whole damn neighborhood with gunshots, the cops might show up before they could get away.

Whoever the guy was, he was no whiz at picking locks. The shadowy form stayed at the door and the tapping sound continued.

Diesel cocked his head as he stared at the door. He whispered, "Something ain't right."

"What do you mean?" Scooter said, also in a whisper.

Diesel moved closer to the door, then used his own knife to point at it. "When I nod my head, unlock the door and pull it open."

Scooter tiptoed his way up to the door, placed one hand on the lock, and held his knife up high, ready to strike. When the nod came from Diesel, he undid the lock, grabbed the doorknob, then ripped open the door. A form drifted inside and Scooter plunged his blade into it. He realized at once that he had speared a piece of cardboard. The cardboard had been cut to mimic the silhouette of a man and attached to the door with a piece of tape. The breeze outside had been pushing it against the door, which is what had made the tapping sound they had been hearing. The cardboard stayed erect, supported by Scooter's blade. Scooter slammed the door shut and freed his knife.

"What the hell?"

Someone whistled. The sound came from the doorway leading into the kitchen. Diesel and Scooter turned to see Tanner pointing a gun at them. The gun had a sound suppressor attached.

Diesel was moving as the sound of Tanner's whistling still lingered in the air. He was betting he was quick enough to bury his blade into Tanner before the man could fire off a shot. He was right, well, almost.

While his speed was uncanny, he was not the only one in the world possessed of such gifts. Tanner belonged to that class of men. He dropped to the floor, rolled, and took Diesel's feet out from under him. Diesel's blade had missed Tanner by only inches before he tripped over Tanner and went to the floor. The impact of his huge body hitting the floor shook the house.

Diesel was getting his feet beneath him when Tanner rose to his knees and sent a shot into the behemoth's side. Diesel grunted, lunged toward Tanner, and received a second bullet to the face. The back of his head erupted in gore as the round exited. The body was still falling when Tanner spun toward Scooter. Scooter hadn't moved. He was standing by the rear door with his mouth hanging open in shock, having witnessed Diesel's death. When he recovered, he shouted at Tanner.

"You're a dead man! Dead. You just killed one of

Lucifer's Angels. Our whole damn club will hunt you down and kill you."

Tanner sent a round into Scooter's right knee. His threats stopped and his moaning began as the wounded knee drove him to the floor. Tanner took away the knives and the phones they had, along with the guns they'd had stuffed at their backs, in their waistbands. He then left Scooter and headed upstairs to see if there was anyone else in the house. On his way there, he saw that the door leading down to the basement was locked with a steel bolt that could only be unlatched from his side. After returning to the first floor, he found Scooter wiping away tears of pain as blood dripped from his wounded knee.

Scooter interested Tanner. His slim build matched that of the person he had seen driving the car on the night Tonya had been killed. He could have also been the man Michael Hallam's neighbor had seen, the one who had been wearing a yellow hoodie.

"What's your name?"

"You go to hell."

Tanner walked over and kicked the knee he'd shot earlier. Scooter's mouth opened in a silent scream as he clenched his eyes shut against the pain.

Tanner tried asking another question once the agony had subsided.

"Did you kill Michael Hallam?"

Scooter managed a smile. "Go to hell."

Another kick and another scream, one that produced a howl and made Scooter's eyes flicker, as a cold sweat ran down his thin face. Tanner wondered if he was going to pass out, but the slim man managed to remain conscious.

"Did you kill Tonya Wilson while driving Michael Hallam's car?"

There was no smile this time, and Scooter was gasping

as if he had been running, but he managed two words of defiance.

"Fuck… you."

After speaking, Scooter hunched his shoulders, anticipating another kick to his damaged knee. He received a bullet instead. It struck him between the eyes, and his body went limp, to fall back against a wall. If Scooter had been the man who'd killed Tonya, Tanner had gotten his revenge.

He tossed the phones and the knives he had taken onto the kitchen floor as he headed out the way he had come in, through the front door. He wasn't concerned about leaving fingerprints behind; he'd been wearing a pair of thin gloves.

Tanner would have to approach Hayward using a different method. He was back in Manhattan and waiting outside the door of an establishment that sold men's clothing. He had some shopping to do before he spoke to Hayward. He intended to do so in a place where the man would not be expecting him.

It was a beautiful summer day in the city of New York, one that Tonya would miss, as she would miss many other things her killer had deprived her of ever experiencing.

Scooter hadn't killed her. Tanner sensed that to be true. Tonya's murderer was still out there, somewhere. When he found him, Tanner would make him pay in kind.

Tanner sighed, feeling the ache of Tonya's absence. He figured some part of him would feel her loss forever.

GUESS WHO'S COMING TO LUNCH

Brent Hayward was not having a good day, and it wasn't yet nine a.m.

He'd been on his way to work when Archer called him and let him know that the two men Steelman had left in Brooklyn to kill Tanner had been murdered. That told Hayward that Tanner was more of a threat than he'd imagined.

When he arrived at Dangal Corp's headquarters, he stayed inside his limo so he could meet with Archer in private to give him new instructions. He was no longer willing to rely on Steelman's thugs to solve the problem. One thing Hayward had learned in business was that it was vital to match the right person with a job that needed doing. Steelman's people had failed once. He wasn't willing to risk a second failure against a man who killed so easily.

"Hire a hit man?" Archer said. "I wouldn't know how to go about it."

"I assumed that, but we know men who will know how. Talk to those ex-cons we have disrupting that union. I'm certain one of them will place you on the right track."

"All right. What's the budget for this project?"

"I'm tempted to lowball it. After all, how difficult can it be to murder one man? However, something is telling me not to be penny-wise and pound-foolish. Use a budget of twenty-thousand dollars, but for that much money I'll want someone with a proven record and a sterling reputation for getting the job done, not some hood with a scoped rifle."

"Understood. I would point out that the expense might not be needed. Steelman sounded enraged over his men being killed. He stated he was coming to New York to hunt their killer down."

"And just how will he go about that? We don't even have a name for the man yet."

"True, but Steelman will be motivated to find the man and eliminate him."

"I still want to hire a pro. If we find one who handles our problem, I may keep the man on retainer."

"I'll get right on it and give you an update over lunch."

"Yes. What else is on the schedule for today?"

"Kevin and Kelly both called me last night. They want us to hire a lawyer for them. They insist they are innocent and never killed those pimps."

"Ignore them. They've become useless. With the charges and the evidence against them, they'll be old men if they ever get released from prison. What else is there?"

Archer went on to update his boss on the progress their other operatives were making in the assignments they had been given.

"And oh yes, Dustin Evans is unavailable. Someone gave him a beating. From the description he provided me, I think it was the same man Kevin and Kelly encountered."

Hayward was nodding. "I see my instincts were right. The man needs to be handled. Hire a professional killer, spend as much as twenty-five thousand if you need to. I can't have everything I've built threatened by the actions of one man."

"I'll handle it," Archer said.

∾

THE TWO WENT UPSTAIRS AND SETTLED INTO THEIR USUAL routines of work, with Archer having the extra and unusual chore of having to hire an assassin.

Hayward's mood brightened around noon when he received word through Archer from one of his corporate spies. She was a young woman working as an executive assistant at a corporation that had a division involved in providing financial advice to accredited investors. Such individuals had an income in excess of two hundred thousand dollars or a net worth of over a million dollars.

That same division of the corporation frequently reinvested their own profits in the stock market. With their connections, they often became aware of mergers and acquisitions that could affect the price of certain stocks.

Hayward's spy had learned about a decision that had been made to attempt a hostile takeover of another financial services company by making a tender offer. That company's stock was currently trading at twelve dollars a share, an offer price of thirty dollars a share was going to be tendered to their board in two days' time.

Knowing many of the players on that company's board personally, as well as the chairman who he had gone to Princeton with, Hayward was certain they would agree to be bought out. He called his broker and told him to buy ten thousand shares of the stock. When the hostile takeover began, his stock would soar and make him a small fortune.

That was one reason he was smiling when he left for

lunch with Archer at his side. Another reason for the smile was the anticipation of his meal. He was going to his favorite restaurant and planned to indulge his sweet tooth. Not only did they serve fine French cuisine, but they also offered delicate pastries. He'd have to put in an extra hour or two on the treadmill to keep from gaining weight, but he deemed it worth the effort.

They were seated at his usual table. Both Hayward and Archer ordered *Concombre a la Menthe*, cucumber salad with mint, as an appetizer. Archer ordered his usual *Croque Monsieur*, which was a glorified ham and cheese sandwich, but Hayward had been craving *Salmon en papillote* with a side of *Potatoes Dauphinoise*.

They had finished their salads along with half a glass of wine each when Haywood asked Archer if he'd made any headway into hiring an assassin. As coincidence would have it, an assassin took a seat beside Hayward a moment later.

It was Tanner.

He was dressed in a suit as fine as the one Hayward was wearing, along with a watch that cost more than most people made in a year. He fit in with the restaurant's clientele and few gave him a second look. Of those who did look, it was Tanner's unique eyes that had attracted their attention.

Hayward puzzled over the sudden appearance of the well-dressed man seated to his left and asked a question.

"Have we met before?"

"We would have met this morning if you had spent the night in that house in Brooklyn."

It took Hayward a moment to catch the reference. Once he had, he leaned away from Tanner.

"Relax, Hayward. I'm here to talk, not kill."

Archer had noticed the change in his boss's mood. "What's going on? Who are you, sir?"

"My name is Tanner. I was dating Tonya Wilson when she was run down and killed like a mongrel in the street. When I find out who did that, then I'll be ready to kill."

"You mean… you're the one who killed those bikers?"

A waiter came over and asked Tanner if he would like a drink. The man did so by speaking French. It was what his snooty customers expected. When Tanner not only understood the waiter, but answered his query in perfect French, ordering a single malt Scotch, Hayward blinked in surprise. Tanner's style of dress, obvious intelligence, and sophistication had the effect of calming him.

"You're here to talk. That's good. I believe you've been operating under a misapprehension, Tanner. I had nothing to do with Tonya's death, nor do I have any knowledge of anyone else's involvement."

Tanner had stared at Hayward as he spoke. His steady gaze unnerved many men, Hayward was one of them, but he forced himself to maintain eye contact, not wanting Tanner to believe he was lying.

Tanner turned his gaze on Archer. "Who are you?"

"My-my name is James Archer. I'm Mr. Hayward's personal assistant."

"That means you know his secrets. Did he have Tonya killed?"

"No! I swear it. We were both shocked when we learned of her death, and equally shocked upon learning that Michael Hallam had been accused of driving the car that struck her."

"Hallam didn't do it. And someone tried to make it look like he committed suicide afterwards. Hayward here pays people to arrange accidents like the one Tonya had, or to stage suicides. I met two of them this morning."

Hayward held up his right hand as if he were about to give testimony in a court of law.

"I swear to you that I was not responsible for Tonya's death, or of staging Mike Hallam's suicide. I also have information you should know."

"Does it concern Tonya's death?"

"No. It concerns your health. Those men you killed were members of a gang of bikers that have twenty or so members. They won't rest until they take revenge out on you for killing their friends. When that happens, I want you to understand I have nothing to do with it."

"Of course, you're involved, Hayward. You hired those men to kill me. Or did you think I'd forget that?"

Hayward tried a smile. Tried and failed. "We weren't acquainted then. Had I known you were a reasonable man, we would have sat across from each other sooner and talked things out as we're doing now."

Tanner's whiskey was delivered to the table. He ignored it and kept staring at Hayward.

"Let's say that I believe you had no reason to want Tonya dead. What about the biker gang? Would they have had a reason to want her dead?"

"I can't think of any. Tonya had no connection to them. Are you certain she wasn't killed by Mike Hallam, as everyone thought? It was his car that struck her. Perhaps whoever tried to make his death look like a suicide did so for a motive that had nothing to do with Tonya's death."

"Hallam slept with a woman when he was drunk, then told his wife about it, but he never mentioned the woman's name. Do you know who she might have been?"

Hayward shrugged. "I can't imagine. But there are dozens of good-looking women working for Dangal Corp. It could have been almost anyone of them, even—never mind."

"You were going to say that it might have been Tonya. I've thought of that. It wasn't her. The timing isn't right. On the night Hallam slept with the woman, Tonya had been with me."

Archer cleared his throat before speaking. "I know we're not being helpful, Mr. Tanner, but we really know nothing about it. You can see that, can't you? And that there is no need for further violence."

"I won't kill either of you unless I find out you're lying. I will kill anyone who comes after me, and then I'll kill the men who sent them. That includes you, Hayward."

"I don't control Steelman or his gang, Tanner. You shouldn't have killed his men."

Tanner stood. "No. Someone shouldn't have killed Tonya. And I will find out who that was."

After Tanner left the restaurant, Hayward called Steelman while using Archer's phone.

"If you're calling to tell me you had an uninvited guest for lunch, don't bother. I already know about it."

Hayward looked around the restaurant, imagining he would see Steelman sitting at the bar or a table. The mad brute would look as out of place as a rhino in a rose garden.

"How do you know about Tanner?"

"Shit, is this Hayward? I thought your pet preppy was calling me."

"I'm using Archer's phone."

"You asked me about Tanner. Is that the name of the dude that killed my men?"

"That's what he said."

"Good. They can write it on his tombstone."

"Are you nearby? Have you been watching me?"

"Not me. But I did hire two pros to deal with this

Tanner. He'll be dead sometime this afternoon. Count on it."

"You hired a professional killer? I had the same idea."

"I hired two people. They're not usually hired killers, but shit happens, and they're not squeamish about it when it does."

"I don't understand what you mean."

"And you don't need to. What you do need to do is to reimburse me for the two men I lost."

"Why would I do that? Your men knew the risk they were taking."

"Hayward, you either pay me twenty grand each for my men and another twenty for killing Tanner, or I swear you will be one sorry son of a bitch. Do you read me?"

Hayward gripped the phone tighter. "I understand. You'll be reimbursed."

"Damn right. And once Tanner is dead, we can get back to business as usual."

"How reliable are these men you've hired? Have they ever failed?"

"They're not men; they're women."

"Women? Against a man like Tanner? Have you seen him? He's... intimidating."

"Is he huge like me?"

"Not at all, but there's something formidable about him."

"That won't matter. He'll die like anyone else. And listen, I'll want my money when he's dead."

"You'll have it."

"If I don't, you'll be the next one to die."

The call ended and Hayward passed the phone back to Archer.

"Have you hired an assassin yet?"

"I've made contact with one. The man has an excellent

reputation and a dozen years of experience. I'm waiting for him to get back to me. Should I cease my efforts? From your end of the conversation, it sounds like Steelman will be handling the Tanner problem."

"No. Hire the hit man anyway. We'll use him against Tanner if needed, and if not, I may have an alternate target for the man to kill."

"You're talking about Steelman?"

"The thug threatened me. I think our association needs to end. Once he's dead, whoever takes his place as leader of the motorcycle gang may be more respectful."

"Did I hear you right? Has Steelman hired two women to go up against Tanner?"

"That's what he said. Imagine what beasts they must be for him to have such faith in them."

The entrees arrived. The salmon smelled delicious, but Hayward's appetite and good mood had been ruined.

17

LIGHTS OUT

THE WOMEN STEELMAN HIRED TO KILL TANNER WERE anything but beasts, as Hayward had imagined. They were two gorgeous young women who could be as deadly as they were beautiful.

Their names were Judi Frost and Darlene Briggs. They were both twenty-five and had known each other since birth.

They weren't assassins by trade; they were con artists and thieves, but as Steelman said, shit happens. The women often used drugs as a method to disable their victims so they could rob them. More than one man had died after having an adverse reaction to the sedative they used, or they were given more than they should have.

Everyone died eventually. If they died while being robbed, then oh well, as far as Judi and Darlene were concerned.

Judi was a tall blonde with small breasts and a face so beautiful that men found it difficult not to stare. Darlene was just as attractive. She had long, dark hair and an abundance of curves in all the right places. While not as

115

tall as Judi, who was five-feet-ten, Darlene shared her eye color, which was turquoise. In certain light their eyes appeared blue, at other times, in different lighting conditions, they could be described as green. Darlene's father had the same eyes. Judi and Darlene suspected they might be half-sisters. They knew for a fact that Darlene's father and Judi's mother had been involved in an affair.

Darlene was more intelligent and made the decisions for them.

It was Darlene who'd decided they should both run away from home at seventeen after quitting high school. They had grown up in a suburb of Memphis, Tennessee. Their families had been close in some respects, since Judi's mother and father both worked for Darlene's father. Judi's mother had dated Darlene's father in high school. He'd broken up with her when he went away to college in a different state.

Judi suspected her mother had never gotten over Darlene's father and had been sleeping with him for decades behind her father's back. If so, it would explain how she got the turquoise eyes, given that her parents' eyes were both brown.

If her father ever discovered the truth, she didn't know. She did know the man never showed much interest in her. Judi had never missed her parents after running away from home and she doubted either of them had missed her.

Darlene's mother had likely been frantic with worry, but Darlene had disliked the woman because her mother had always tried to control her. The two were much alike, as Darlene enjoyed being in control as well.

When she accepted the contract on Tanner, it was with the anticipation of humbling an obviously capable alpha male type. She hated such men. Her father was one. All her father ever cared about was making his next million dollars or buying a bigger house to impress people and swell his already inflated ego. Jack Briggs swaggered through life thinking he was unstoppable. He'd been captain of his high school football team, played on a team that won a national championship in college, and had received offers to play pro football. He had declined the offers because he'd wanted a career in business, the family business, Briggs Automotive. Darlene's grandfather had inherited a used car lot from his father and had built it into a chain of six new car dealerships.

Darlene's father, Jack Briggs, had brought that number up to eleven while also expanding into auto supply stores. He acted as if he were a self-made man instead of someone who'd been born on third base.

Darlene had grown to hate her father as she was growing up. The man was a misogynist, and as controlling as her mother was, the woman would never talk back to her father. Darlene suspected that her mother felt like a failure because she had only been able to give the great Jack Briggs a daughter instead of a son. But they'd kept trying for that son, as six miscarriages could testify. Eventually, the doctors warned her mother against getting pregnant again.

Darlene was sure her father had a son somewhere with another woman, just as he had likely fathered Judi because of an affair.

She loved targeting men who reminded her of her father. And not all of the overdoses that killed their victims had been accidental. They traveled around the country picking up successful men in bars, drugging them, then robbing them. There was also blackmail involved, as they sometimes took photos of the men lying naked in bed with them. Of course, such photos never revealed *their* faces, only the faces of their victims.

A successful man would often send a reasonable monthly fee to an account in a foreign bank if it meant avoiding a messy divorce that could cost him half his net worth or sully his reputation.

Tanner wouldn't be a target of blackmail. He was to be killed. Period. Steelman had told Judi and Darlene that Tanner was interested in a man named Brent Hayward, and that he would probably make contact with Hayward within a day or two. The man had been right, but Darlene had nearly been fooled by Tanner's expensive suit. At first, she had thought he was a business associate of Hayward's who had stopped by his table to chat. But then she saw the expression on Hayward's face. Fear had flashed across that handsome face like the shadow of a bird of prey. Meanwhile, Hayward's assistant had briefly worn an expression of terror. Darlene knew that look. It was how a man looked when he feared he was about to be killed.

And then there were the eyes. Steelman hadn't been able to give them a name for their target, but he did have a basic description of the man that had been given to him by Hayward, whose people had met the man.

Intense eyes, scary eyes, and yeah, the man who sat down at Hayward's table had scary eyes.

And he's as sexy as hell too, Darlene had thought.

She and Judi had followed Hayward to the restaurant, then Darlene had gone inside to take a seat at the bar. Since she was following around a businessman, she herself was dressed in business attire. She wore a belted skirt dress with a hemline that fell just above her knees. The top of the dress above the belt was white with black polka dots, while the bottom was all black. The red high heels she wore made her appear even taller than she was.

When Tanner left the restaurant, Darlene followed on foot while Judi stayed close with the car. After spotting him getting into a vehicle of his own, Darlene joined Judi in the car and kept Tanner in sight. He hadn't gone far, and after paying to leave his car in an underground parking lot, he emerged and entered a bar that was across the street, an Irish pub.

"What do we do now?" Judi asked.

"He might remember me from the restaurant and think it odd that I wound up in the same bar as him. You go inside and pick him up."

"We'll need a room to bring him to."

Darlene pointed across the street, where there was a hotel that catered to tourists.

"That will do. We'll rent a room and then you make your move."

"I wish this was real. I would not mind spending time in bed with that man."

"I know, right, but work is work, so don't let your guard down. The man is dangerous."

Darlene's phone beeped, telling her she had a text.

"Ah, Steelman knows the man's name now. He calls himself Tanner."

"The cops will be calling him a homicide victim soon."

The women donned hats with wide brims before entering the hotel to get a room. The hats would keep their faces from being picked up by the hotel's cameras. They were given a room on the third floor that offered a view of the street. That worked out well, for it would allow Darlene to keep the entrance to the bar in sight. She would keep watch and know when Judi was bringing Tanner back to the room. She never doubted that Judi would seduce the man. With their good looks and southern accents, neither of them had ever been turned down.

Judi left to walk over to the bar. While she was gone, Darlene prepared a hypodermic needle by filling it with a fast-acting poison. Once the drug was injected into Tanner, he would be dead in seconds.

～

TANNER SAW JUDI ENTER THE BAR AND LOOK AROUND. When her eyes met his, she smiled at him in a shy manner before looking away. He was seated at the bar and having a burger and beer. Judi settled two stools away, placed her hat on the bar, and ordered a glass of white wine. She was wearing a blue skirt that rode up to mid-thigh as she sat, to expose her shapely legs.

A man farther down the bar left his seat and moved over to talk to Judi, by taking the stool to her left. He was about forty-five and dressed in jeans and a sports jacket that was a vibrant shade of blue. He'd left a thick case behind where he'd been sitting. Tanner pegged him as a salesman. The salesman was trying to reel in a new customer, but Judi wasn't interested, and made that fact known in short order.

"I said no. I don't want you to buy me a drink. And don't think I didn't see you remove your wedding band."

The salesman knew a tough customer when he saw one. He grabbed up his sample case, waved to the bartender and went back out onto the mean streets of Manhattan.

Judi spoke to Tanner. "I'm sorry about the raised voice. I hope I didn't disturb your meal?"

"You didn't," Tanner said, then he told the bartender to give the lady another drink.

Judi grinned at him. "That's the way to do it. Just buy a lady a drink without asking for permission."

"I could always apologize later if you refused the drink."

Judi slid over one seat, settling next to Tanner. "What's your name?"

"I'm Tanner."

"I'm Judi, Tanner. Thank you for the drink."

They talked for a while, with Judi laughing often. After finishing her third glass of wine, she leaned over and kissed Tanner on the lips.

"You're very attractive. I'd like to spend some time with you alone."

"That can be arranged."

"I have a room nearby and I'll only be in the city for a few days. It would be nice to leave here with some pleasant memories."

Tanner stood, while tossing money on the bar. "Let's go make those memories."

~

Darlene whispered, "Yes," as she watched Judi leave the bar with Tanner. She was looking forward to seeing the shocked expression on the man's face when he realized he'd been fooled, that he wasn't cock of the walk, and that a woman had tricked him.

She would daydream sometimes about returning home to Tennessee and killing her father. She would torture the bastard first for good measure. The man had never even considered bringing her into the family business as he had been. No, she was expected to "Marry a good man someday, like your mother did with me."

There were no good men as far as Darlene was concerned, least of all her sexist and misogynistic father.

Darlene watched Judi and Tanner until she could no longer see them. After grabbing the syringe, she stood by the door, and waited. The elevator was nearby. When she heard it make a *Ding!* sound upon its arrival, she looked out through the peephole.

～

TANNER HAD BEEN LOOKING DOWN AT JUDI'S WELL-rounded ass when he saw movement at the base of the door Judi had paused in front of. Someone was already in the room. He felt like cursing. He'd been looking forward to spending time with Judi, but the woman was a thief, and there was likely a male partner waiting inside the room to knock him over the head so they could take his cash and credit cards.

He decided to play along, but he'd be changing the rules of their game.

Judi used a key card to unlock the door, then looked over her shoulder at Tanner. "Come on in, lover. I can't wait to get you in bed."

Tanner followed, but ducked down as he crossed the threshold. He kept going, transitioned into a shoulder roll that took him past Judi, and sprang up with his gun in his hand.

Judi and Darlene stood together in front of the door, which was closing after being slammed shut by Darlene. Darlene's right hand was still raised and gripping the syringe with the poison in it. Turquoise eyes widened with surprise as she took in the gun pointed at her.

Judi wore a look of panic, then opened her mouth to scream for help, knowing that someone would hear and come running to investigate. The scream never left her mouth, but part of a front tooth did. Tanner had kicked her in the face to stifle the scream. Judi was sent backwards and hit her head against the door, then slid down it, and sat on the carpet with her chin resting on her chest. She was out cold.

Darlene grunted as she thrust the needle at Tanner and missed. She then hit the floor as Tanner took her feet out from under her with a sweep kick that struck her left ankle. The syringe left her hand and fell on top of her, landing on her neck. The look of panic in her eyes told Tanner that there might be something lethal contained in the vial. Instead of thieves, he was dealing with fellow assassins.

He knelt beside Darlene and slammed an elbow into the side of her head. She was tougher than she looked, so he did it again, and it was lights out.

18

A TRIP TO THE WOODS

Darlene regained consciousness and found herself lying on the bed inside the hotel room, to the right of Judi, who was still unconscious.

Their wrists and ankles were bound with strips of cloth, and their mouths had been gagged. The cloth was white. When she saw an uncovered pillow lying on the floor, Darlene realized Tanner had cut a pillowcase into strips to bind them.

Tanner stood by the window, looking out. When he sensed her moving, he turned to look at her, then he held up the syringe.

"What's in here? I'm guessing it would have killed me if I'd given you the chance to use it."

Darlene shook her head while mumbling.

"Okay. If it wouldn't have killed me, then I guess it won't kill you either."

Tanner approached her and positioned the syringe above Darlene's right thigh. Her mumbling increased as she struggled to get away. There was nowhere to go, not with Tanner on one side and Judi on the other.

125

"Yeah. That's what I thought. This thing is full of poison."

Darlene began crying. The tears were real as she was terrified. No mark had ever turned the tables on them before. She hoped Tanner was the sort of man who was softened by a woman's tears, but she doubted it.

Judi had revived. She looked around in confusion before recalling what had happened. Tears appeared in her eyes as well, when she saw that Tanner held the syringe. Since Judi had seemed more inclined to scream than Darlene, Tanner freed the gag around Darlene's mouth.

She had to spit out a wad of pillowcase before she could talk.

"Don't kill us."

"Why shouldn't I? You were going to kill me."

Judi mumbled, wanting to be heard. Tanner warned her against screaming and freed her gag. As Darlene had done, she spat out her gag, then used her tongue to probe at her front teeth.

"I have part of a tooth missing up front," Judi said. And there was a whistling sound when she said the word missing.

"Who hired you two to kill me?"

"No one," Judi said. "We just wanted to rob you."

"Lie to me again and I'll inject you. Who hired you?"

"Steelman. A biker guy named Steelman," Darlene said.

Tanner was surprised. Using two beautiful women to kill him seemed more like something Hayward would have done, and he remembered having seen Darlene inside the restaurant.

"Where can I find Steelman?"

"He met us at an Italian hot dog stand out on Route 22

in Scotch Plains, New Jersey. I don't know where he normally is."

"What else do you know about him, or about Hayward?"

"Nothing," Judi said.

He gazed down at Judi. Her skirt had ridden up nearly to the level of her crotch.

Judi had taken notice of where he was looking. "Hey, Tanner. We could still have fun, you know? You don't have to hurt us."

"I think I'll pass. It wouldn't be the same. It would feel too much like rape. I'm not a rapist."

"But you are a killer," Darlene said. "Steelman said you murdered two of his men."

"I did. They were trying to kill me. That's what I do to people who try to kill me; I kill them first."

Tanner took out a folding knife and heard both women gasp. He opened the knife and placed it in Darlene's right hand.

"I'll kill you both if I ever see you again."

After carefully wrapping the syringe in a strip of the pillowcase, Tanner left the room carrying the needle of death.

~

IT HAD TAKEN DARLENE EIGHT MINUTES TO FREE HER wrists with the knife, while also opening a small cut on the back of her hand. After freeing herself, she released Judi from her bonds.

They left the hotel in a rush while looking around warily. They didn't want to risk Tanner changing his mind and returning. When they reached their rental, Judi cried out in frustration.

"Oh, I can't find the damn key. Let me have yours."

Darlene passed her the key, and they climbed into the car.

"That's as close as I ever want to get to dying," Judi said.

Darlene's reply sounded muffled. When Judi turned her head to look at her, she saw she had a hand clamped over her mouth. There was also a needle being withdrawn from her neck. The hand covering Darlene's mouth and the one holding the syringe both belonged to Tanner.

Judi made a cry of distress, opened her door, and attempted to leap from the car. She had forgotten that she had fastened her seat belt. Tanner reached over and shut the door before covering her mouth and injecting her.

He wasn't sure if whatever was in the syringe was powerful enough to kill both women, but their reactions assured him of success. The drug worked fast, more so on Judi than on Darlene. Judi slumped in her seat and would have fallen onto the steering wheel if not for the seat belt holding her in place. It was only a few seconds later that she stopped breathing.

Darlene sagged against her door. Her mouth moved, but no words came out. Tanner stared at her, waiting for her to die.

DARLENE HAD BEEN ATTEMPTING TO BEG FOR MERCY THAT didn't exist. Then she remembered what Tanner had told them.

"That's what I do to people who try to kill me; I kill them first."

Darlene died with those words echoing in her mind.

~

TANNER WOULD HAVE KILLED THE WOMEN INSIDE THE hotel room if he hadn't been seen and caught on camera in the bar and the hotel with Judi.

When he was certain they were both dead, he moved Judi onto the rear bench seat and reclined the back of the passenger seat Darlene occupied. There were sunglasses in their purses. He placed them on them. To a casual observer, they would appear to be asleep.

An hour later, he was in a section of woods north of the city and starting work on a grave, after having stopped to buy a shovel, lime, and a roll of plastic, along with a butterfly bush he was told would, "Blossom into a nice red color."

He'd only bought the bush so it wouldn't seem odd that he'd purchased the other items. However, after digging a grave for Judi and Darlene, Tanner planted the bush on top of it.

When he was finished, he drove their car back to the city and left it in the parking lot of one of the rental agency's locations it had come from. It would seem odd that the customer had just dropped the car off that way, but the rental company would already have payment information on record. As long as they weren't losing money, they wouldn't make a fuss and involve the cops.

Afterward, Tanner retrieved his own car and returned to his hotel room, showered, then changed into fresh clothes. He had worked up an appetite digging a grave deep enough to hold two women, so he decided to go across the street to the place that sold pizza. He was reaching for the door handle when he changed his mind. The lovely Judi had left him with another appetite he wanted to satisfy.

After getting back in his car, he drove to the bar where he had been with Thaxton. The blonde waitress was there, the one who had taken a liking to him.

When she got off work, Tanner drove her home. As they entered her apartment, no one tried to jab him in the neck with a needle full of poison.

Judi had promised him sex with the intent to kill him. The pretty waitress only wanted to give him pleasure. Tanner left her bed the next morning with a promise to call her soon. But first, he had a group of bikers to hunt down. Hunt down and kill.

19

A HUNTING HE WILL GO

Thaxton heard the door on his outer office open and wondered if he had a new client come to call on him. The woman who answered his phones and did his paperwork greeted their guest, and Thaxton recognized the man's voice when he answered. It was Tanner.

Thaxton walked over to stand in the doorway of his office and gestured for Tanner to join him inside.

"It's okay, Maggie. He doesn't need to make an appointment."

Tanner entered the office, and Thaxton shut the door.

"Two members of the Lucifer's Devils Motorcycle Club were found dead yesterday in Brooklyn. Would you know anything about that?"

"You're an ex-cop, right Thaxton?"

"I am."

"I won't be answering that question."

"You will if Colleen, Detective Blum, asks you. And she'll do the asking inside an interrogation room."

"That's why I haven't bothered talking to her. Besides,

the police have listed Tonya's death as a hit-and-run. They're not interested in knowing the truth; they only want to improve their crime statistics by labeling it an accident instead of murder."

"There's merit in what you say, but Detective Blum isn't like that. It's why she asked me to keep digging for the truth when she can't."

"The truth is that someone killed Tonya. When I find out who that is, I will kill them."

Thaxton settled behind his desk and asked Tanner to take a seat in one of his two wooden client chairs. Tanner did so, then revealed the reason for his visit.

"I need to find out where the biker gang's headquarters is. I was hoping you could help me with that."

"Why, so you can kill them?"

"That's another question I won't answer."

"I'll take it as a yes whenever you say that. But Tanner, this is a gang we're talking about. I've already looked into them. They have somewhere around twenty members—with two less now—and they make their home in Camden, New Jersey, which has one of the highest crime rates in the country. I'm sure this biker gang is responsible for at least some of that. The gang is suspected of running drugs, dealing in illegal weapons, and committing contract murders. A few of the members have gone down for petty violations that get them six months or a year in jail, but so far, none have taken a hard fall."

"Do you have an address for them?"

"No. I'm not sure I'd give it to you if I did. If you go up against these guys, you could get yourself killed."

"One of them was hired to kill your client's wife."

"I think you're right. I don't know how I'll ever prove it."

"I have an idea about that. I'll get you your proof, if it

works out." Tanner stood and headed for the door, then he turned around to give advice. "Watch your back, Thaxton. If the wrong people learn you're sniffing around this, they could target you for death."

"I can take care of myself. It's you I'm worried about. You're going to Camden, aren't you?"

"That's one more question I won't answer."

"Damn it, Tanner. Don't get yourself killed. I never met the woman, but I'm sure Tonya Wilson wouldn't want you risking your life to get revenge for her murder."

Tanner left Thaxton's office and headed to an underground parking garage where he kept a stash of weapons, clothing, and a fake ID.

He made his way to the rear of the facility, where he retrieved a hidden key behind a loose brick. He used the key to open the back doors of a gray panel van.

The windows were heavily tinted, while the windshield was covered with a cardboard sunshade, which blocked a view of the vehicle's interior. The sunshade was taped tightly to the front window and reinforced beneath by black plastic.

Tanner climbed in through the rear, closed and locked the doors, then put on a light. The interior of the van held guns, ammo, clothing, medical supplies, equipment, and even food and water.

It was one of three such weapon and supply caches he had hidden about the city, and they were used to rearm and restock. He had two other weapon caches back in the Las Vegas area. In a pinch, he could also sleep in the vans, although not well, because of the restraints of space.

After choosing a case that contained a sniper rifle. He grabbed a scope that had thermal capability, along with a device he could use to charge it using his car's cigarette lighter. Tanner also grabbed two boxes of ammunition, totaling a hundred rounds, along with a bulletproof vest.

Steelman, the leader of Lucifer's Angels, had made two attempts to kill him. It was time Tanner fought back.

He loaded his supplies into his car and headed south, toward New Jersey.

REAP THE WHIRLWIND

CAMDEN, NEW JERSEY, IS LOCATED ACROSS THE DELAWARE River from Philadelphia, Pennsylvania. It boasts a population of over seventy-one thousand, many of whom could trace their families back for generations. It began as a fur trading post in 1626. In modern times, bags of drugs were often traded for cash on the city's streets, something hardly unique in urban areas.

The trip to Camden had taken Tanner just over two hours. During his first hour, he made the crime rate rise by stealing an old car from a used car lot and acquired license plates from another vehicle. He needed transportation he could abandon if it became necessary. But first, he had to track down Steelman's motorcycle gang.

He began his search by visiting bars and the few places that repaired motorcycles. He was hoping to spot a member of the motorcycle club. Unlike mafia members, those in gangs liked to play dress up and wear certain colors or clothing that identified them as a member of their gang. Motorcycle club members, in particular, tended to wear the name of their group on the backs of leather vests or jackets. One of the men he had killed in Brooklyn, Scooter, had been wearing such a vest, so Tanner knew what to look for.

The back of Scooter's vest had the words, Lucifer's Devils, written over the image of a grinning, red Devil's head with prominent horns. The other man, Diesel, had the same thing tattooed on his left arm.

Tanner was searching for that image. He refrained from asking anyone about the motorcycle club because you never knew who you were talking to. They could be a friend of someone inside the club or a family member who would warn them that someone was looking for them.

Asking about Steelman and his group would also make Tanner memorable. He didn't need that, not when he was in the city to commit mass murder. Lucifer's Angels had tried to kill him twice. It was time they learned the price for attacking a Tanner.

He was stopped for gas on Ferry Avenue and about to leave the station when he heard the sound of motorcycles nearby. A pair of them sped past close enough for Tanner to get a good look at them and spot the grinning, red Devil heads on the rear of their vests.

Tanner followed from a short distance and kept them in view. He was wondering if they were headed somewhere out of the city as they approached the border of the next town, Pennsauken, but then they exited the highway.

They left the main streets behind and drove along a narrow two-lane road that bordered the Cooper River, then moved inland. Because there was no one else driving in the area, Tanner had to let them leave his sight or he risked being spotted and alerting them of his intentions.

He was still able to determine their direction of travel by the thunderous sounds their motorcycles made.

After rounding a curve at a slow speed, he caught sight

of a large home through the trees and came to a stop. He could no longer hear the motorcycles. The house must have been their destination.

Tanner backed the car up along the road until he reached a dirt track he remembered passing. It might be what remained of a driveway where a home once sat. He thought he might need to camouflage the car; that became unnecessary when the track curved left before ending at a clearing. In that spot, it couldn't be seen from the road.

Tanner left the car and traveled light, with only a handgun. Although it seemed he had located the motorcycle gang, the time wasn't right to act. He needed to gather intelligence before he struck.

The house he'd glimpsed through the trees had been only one of two structures, three if you counted the old, huge wooden sign that was set at the entrance to the property. The sign was faded, the wood splintered, and sagging, but you could still make out the words on it.

MILLER'S TAVERN AND HOTEL

Miller was likely long dead, and his hotel and bar weren't long for this world. It was a big house with three floors that Tanner guessed took up over four thousand square feet. It had been converted into a hotel at some point in the past. The bar, which had once been a small barn or large shed, was a fraction of the size of the house and one end of it had collapsed in on itself, or maybe a tree had come down on it at some point. From the third floor of the home, you would have been able to see the river, and there was a small lake nearby. Miller's must have been a nice place to stay during its heyday. It had become the hideout and headquarters of a motorcycle gang.

There was an old cemetery nearby. Tanner entered it and climbed onto the roof of the caretaker's shack and laid flat. He used a pair of binoculars to study the six members of the motorcycle gang. One of them was huge. The man was damn near seven feet tall and had arms as thick as most men's thighs. After observing the way the other men were interacting with him, Tanner felt certain he was looking at Steelman.

He spent an hour watching the gang and another hour scouting out the area. He decided that the roof of the caretaker's shack was the best spot to shoot from, as there were no hills in the area and none of the trees offered a better line of sight on the old tavern. That tavern was where the men spent most of their time. The hotel was used for sleeping.

Tanner returned to the car he had stolen and checked his watch. It was near four in the afternoon. He would return after dark with the sniper rifle loaded and be ready to act.

WHEN JUDI AND DARLENE FAILED TO CONTACT STEELMAN and confirm they had killed Tanner, the biker had phoned Brent Hayward and told him he owed him more money for the loss of the women. Judi and Darlene hadn't been a part of his gang, as other women were and had been, but they'd been a valuable resource.

Hayward had promised to pay. After the call ended, he phoned Archer and told him to come to his office.

"What's the status of this hit man you've hired?"

"He'll be in the city tomorrow. It cost the whole twenty-five thousand dollars to hire him. That also covered his expenses in traveling here. The man I used to make contact with him says the guy has years of experience and is one of the best."

"Excellent."

"Um, there is one thing you should know."

"And that is?"

"The hit man said he'll need you to draw Tanner out into the open, since you're the one he seems interested in."

Hayward's smile surprised Archer. "That won't be a problem at all. We'll choose a spot that's secluded and lure Tanner in, then that hit man can place a bullet in the pest's head."

"I thought you would balk at placing yourself at risk, sir. It's brave of you to act as bait."

Hayward's smile grew wider. "I won't be at risk." He studied Archer. "You know, from a distance, and in bad lighting, you could be mistaken for me."

Archer swallowed hard, understanding what Hayward wanted him to do.

◠

TANNER RETURNED TO THE SITE NEAR THE RIVER AROUND nine p.m. and saw that there were twenty people present, along with Steelman, who was damn near large enough to have his own zip code. Three of those people were women.

There was a generator running to provide light and refrigeration inside the old bar. Outside, there was a fire burning in a round, wide pit. The short wall of the pit had been made using cobblestones. The men sat around it and drank beer, while women sat among them and laughed at their jokes.

All three of the women had tattoos of the grinning devil on their arms. Tanner had found himself staring at the tattoo on one woman's arm as she had stood in the powerful light given off by a motorcycle's headlamp earlier. It looked to be fresh, brighter than the others. She was fresh and bright as well, and possibly young enough to be underage. Something about the girl's tattoo had captivated Tanner, but he didn't know why.

The girl was with Steelman and stayed close to him. Killing the men with the women so near would make things more difficult, as Tanner had no desire to harm anyone but the male members of the club.

He decided to kill Steelman first. He was their leader and the one who had ordered other people to kill him. If possible, Tanner would kill the other men as well, but knew he needed to allow himself time to get away.

The sound of the shots from the sniper rifle would travel well and would certainly be heard as far back as the highway. If a cop could tell where the shots were coming from, and headed toward the old, dilapidated tavern, Tanner could find himself needing to use the river as a means to escape.

He had prepared for such a contingency. There was a rowboat hidden nearby amid bushes. That was how he'd been trained, to always have a Plan B along with a way to extricate yourself from a situation if things turned bad. It was what his mentor, Spenser, termed due diligence. Such preparation had often meant the difference between success and failure and had saved Tanner's life on more than one occasion.

Tanner waited until everyone was gathered around the firepit and had been drinking for hours. The alcohol would slow their reaction times once he began firing.

He settled himself into a prone position atop the roof of the caretaker's shed inside the cemetery. The firepit was about three hundred yards away. He was sighting in on Steelman when he decided he needed to make a change to his equipment. He had brought along ten-round magazines, but they protruded too far under the gun and would make shooting uncomfortable. Fortunately, he also had the foresight to pack several five-round magazines.

After making the adjustment, and lining up several of the five-round mags within easy reach, he was ready to go to work. Since his work was killing, people were about to die. They were people who would kill him on sight on Steelman's orders, and one of them might have been involved in Tonya's death.

Tanner took aim at Steelman's chest. His finger was tightening on the trigger when Steelman reached over and grabbed the girl who was seated beside him by the neck to give her a rough kiss. The girl was the young one with the fresh tattoo. That had risked placing the girl in the path of death. At the last instant, before the shot was fired, Tanner adjusted his aim a fraction to the right. Instead of striking Steelman in the chest and obliterating his heart, the round tore a chunk out of the outside portion of his left shoulder.

The big man tumbled backwards off the trunk of the fallen tree he'd been seated on and disappeared into the blackness beyond the firelight.

Tanner kept firing. He killed four other men before he needed to pause to reload. He also activated the thermal mode on his optics. That enabled him to see Steelman again. The biker looked like a huge glowing glob through the scope and was moving fast toward the hotel to take cover. Tanner let him go, as the girl was sticking close to Steelman and running on his right. If a round went through the behemoth, there was a risk it could hit the girl afterwards.

There were still plenty of targets. Tanner emptied another magazine and four more of Lucifer's Angels were sent to hell where they belonged. A fifth man suffered a nasty leg wound that blew apart his thigh. It was a safe bet he would bleed out before he'd receive medical care.

Three men fired at Tanner's position after having spotted the flash made by his weapon. Their own weapons were handguns. At three hundred yards, he wasn't out of the range their rounds could reach, but he was far beyond their level of skill. And they were all buzzed. Their rounds missed him to a degree that made their attempts comical. Tanner calmly reloaded again and put the men down one after the other, then shot two more who were running for the motel. Other men had made it inside the building.

The remaining women were standing near the firepit and screaming their heads off as they took in the carnage around them.

Two men returned outside holding rifles. They had improved their firepower considerably, yet they'd gotten no smarter. Tanner shot them dead before either man could get off a single round. One of his rounds passed through a man and hit a motorcycle. It must have penetrated the gas tank as well. The fuel flowed toward the firepit, was ignited by a spark, and flame followed the trail of gas back to the fallen chopper, to set it on fire.

He had killed every man there, with the exception of Steelman. If time weren't a factor, he would have gone inside the hotel and finished the bastard. That couldn't happen. It would place him at risk of being captured by the police. As things stood, he had been there too long already.

Tanner took three seconds to consider the wisdom of using the car to leave the area. He decided against it, left the roof, and headed toward the river. It turned out to be the right decision.

He was paddling away when two police cars came along the two-lane road that dead-ended at the old hotel. Had he used the car, he would have had to abandoned it and taken to the sparse woods.

He headed the boat across the river and landed on the Pennsauken side, near a driving range that was closed for the night.

As part of his preparation, he had left his car parked in the lot of a fast-food restaurant. The place was closing soon, but the drive-thru window was open. Hungry, he stopped to place an order before driving back to where he'd left the boat.

There were flashing lights from four police cars across the river, and the sound of sirens approaching filled the air. At least one of those sirens would belong to an ambulance. The fire department would be called in too. The bike that had caught fire had ignited other motorcycles. Flames from their blaze had sent glowing embers toward the old bar and it was burning. If the fire department didn't arrive soon, the old hotel would go up in flames as well.

Tanner retrieved his rifle and other equipment from the boat and drove away. Steelman would have to be dealt with some other time. For now, he couldn't have more than a man or two left, had his clubhouse burnt down, and was wounded. He had attempted to murder a man who was the best in the world at killing, and he had paid the price.

Brent Hayward would be next.

Tanner chewed on a cheeseburger and sipped on a soda as he made his way back to Manhattan.

IT TAKES A HIT MAN...

Hayward recognized Steelman's gruff voice over the phone the next morning, but the biker's words were uttered in a lackluster manner.

"Say that again?"

"My boys are dead. They're all dead. I think it was this guy Tanner who killed them."

"How the—what?"

"Someone used a sniper rifle on us, and the guy was like a magician with the damn thing. I never got a look at him. I was wounded in the shoulder and then all hell broke loose." A bit of fire returned to Steelman's voice as he next spoke. "Sixteen dead, Hayward. Sixteen guys bought it last night, and that's on top of Diesel and Scooter. My whole club is gone."

Hayward smiled. Tanner was good for something after all. It was too bad he hadn't killed Steelman as well.

"Are you still there?"

"I'm on the line, yes. I was just flabbergasted into speechlessness by what you've told me."

"It gets worse. A fire burned up most of the bikes,

including mine. It also destroyed our headquarters. I want this guy, Tanner, Hayward, and I want him alive, but only so I can kill him myself."

"I can help with that. I've hired an assassin. The man is said to be deadly and has never failed. I suppose he'd be willing to only wound Tanner, so that you could finish him off."

"When is this hitter coming to town?"

"Today. Archer is meeting with him within the hour to make payment and discuss the details. I'll contact him and let him know we only want the man to wound Tanner. It will be my gift to you."

"Tanner is going to be begging to die before I get through with him."

"I'll have to lure him somewhere private. There's a warehouse on the docks that was recently acquired by Dangal Corp. for storage. It's empty right now, and the area is all but deserted at night. Tanner will probably be targeting me next. He can't get to me while I'm inside my office, but I'm sure he'll follow once I leave the building."

"And your hitter will be at that warehouse waiting for him to show?"

"That's right. Tanner will walk right into our trap. I'll have Archer send you the address. Arrive before eight, and Tanner will be yours before nine."

"Oh, I can't wait. I would tear him apart with my own two hands, just rip his damn arms out of their sockets, but I can't. My left arm is in a sling after being wounded."

Hayward rolled his eyes, but he spoke without revealing the disdain he felt for Steelman. "I'm sure you'll come up with something equally as creative when the time arrives."

"The cops here told me not to leave Camden, but screw that. I'll be at that warehouse. Count on it."

The call ended and Hayward sent off a text to Archer

letting him know the change of plans. He would have Tanner wounded instead of killed, but Steelman would never have the pleasure of getting his revenge. Steelman would die at the hands of the hit man he'd hired to kill Tanner.

And with Tanner wounded and easy to handle, Hayward could hand him over to two of the brutes he'd hired to start trouble within the union. They would torture Tanner and get him to talk. Hayward no longer believed Tanner's story about having dated Tonya Wilson and wanting revenge for her death.

It seemed more probable he had been hired by a rival corporation to create havoc. If Tanner really had been dating Tonya, it was likely only as a means to gather information, along with the sex, of course. Tonya Wilson had been one beautiful woman.

Hayward leaned back in his seat and wondered if someone really had killed her. It hadn't been him or any of his people, and he doubted Steelman even knew who she was. If Tonya Wilson had been murdered, it happened for a reason he didn't know.

Archer responded to his text and said that the hit man agreed to the changes he wanted to make.

> What's he like?

He's a bit of a hippie, with long hair.

> I don't care how long his hair is, as long as he gets the job done.

I'll make certain he understands.

The conversation ended, and Hayward stood to look out the window behind the desk. He stiffened and scrambled to lower the blinds after remembering that Steelman said Tanner had used a sniper rifle to kill his bikers.

Hayward spent the rest of the day working in the conference room down the hall from his office, just in case Tanner fired shots through the closed blinds.

It irked him that he feared the man, but he had the good sense to do so.

WOUNDED AND CAPTURED

JAMES ARCHER CLIMBED INTO THE REAR OF HAYWARD'S limo while inside the underground parking garage at Dangal's headquarters. He was at risk of dying and he knew it.

It didn't help to calm his nerves any that the regular driver had been replaced by a thug with a gun, or that a man holding a shotgun was riding in the rear with him. He could still be mistaken for Hayward and killed.

His fear would be greater had he known Tanner had nearly single-handedly wiped-out Lucifer's Angels. He was in a limo, yes, but it was not a bulletproof limo.

How did I let myself be talked into this? Archer wondered, but he knew.

There was nothing he wouldn't do to keep his job. As long as he stayed in the good graces of Brent Hayward, his fortunes could only rise.

Hayward would be running Dangal Corp. someday, and that day wasn't far off. When that happened, as his confidant, he'd undoubtably be given a new title and a massive increase in salary.

And Hayward needed him. He was aware that Archer was able and could be relied upon. Hell, look what he was doing at that very moment. He was pretending to be Hayward in case Tanner decided to kill him before he could be dealt with himself. If that didn't prove his loyalty, then nothing could.

Archer spoke to the limo driver. "Is anyone following us?"

The guy laughed. "We're on Eighth Avenue in New York City. There are a hundred cars following behind us."

"You know what I mean."

"Yeah, yeah. I'll keep an eye out. It will be easier to do once we're near the docks."

Hayward would be at the warehouse ahead of them. He had driven himself there earlier while driving Archer's BMW.

Their hit man would be there too, waiting to go into action. Archer thought twenty-five thousand dollars was a lot of money to receive for killing one man and wounding another. That said, it was something he could never do.

He didn't think he was a coward, but he wasn't brave either, and the thought of shooting someone made him feel queasy. He'd never seen a human being get shot up close, but he had witnessed a dog get killed by a gun.

His grandfather had still been alive when he was six. The man lived on the family farm that was later sold at his death to settle back taxes on the land. His father had left farm life behind because it was too tough. Then the fool wound up working as a day laborer on construction sites up north for most of his life. At least on the farm, he would have been laboring for himself and growing food he could have eaten or sold for a profit.

They had gone back to South Carolina for a visit. Archer had liked the farm, all that open space. He had liked his grandfather too, although he couldn't remember what he looked like now.

He'd been playing outside when a dog appeared. It wasn't his grandfather's old hound, but a stray dog. The beast had been rabid. Being only six at the time, Archer hadn't known what that was and wanted to pet the dog. He was walking toward it when a loud sound came from behind him and the dog in front of him did an odd little flip before falling to the ground.

He couldn't remember his grandfather's face, the man who had fired the shot that had saved him from being bitten, but he'd retained a vivid image of the blood that poured out of the wound a rifle round had created in that dog. After that incident, Archer never liked being around dogs.

He was thinking of that bloody wound from long ago and imagining what it would feel like to have one of his own. The thought made him feel sick. It was a wonder anyone ever survived being shot, which was the rending of their flesh by a hot chunk of steel. A splinter in the meat of his thumb was enough to bring tears to his eyes.

He felt better about things as the trip progressed and nothing happened. If Tanner was going to attack them on the road he might have done so in the first few minutes. That didn't mean he wasn't following them with the intent to commit violence.

TANNER WASN'T FOLLOWING THEM. HE WAS ALREADY AT the warehouse, having learned about the meeting that was to take place.

He'd seen Steelman drive up to the building on a motorcycle that was too small for his huge frame. Tanner supposed it was all Steelman could salvage from the fire that had burned most of the other motorcycles. The man was using only one hand to steer the bike, as his other arm, the left one, was in a sling to aid the healing of his wounded shoulder.

Hayward appeared next. He was driving a BMW instead of being chauffeured around. Tanner had wondered why that was. Assuming all the players were inside already, he was about to step out from the shadows that hid him when Hayward's limousine came down the street. Someone must have been keeping watch for it, as the corrugated metal door of the building's entrance rolled upward again, to let the limo drive on in.

Tanner ran toward the door as it was closing, hit the ground, and rolled beneath it. When he made it to his feet, he did so with his gun in his hand.

His appearance took Steelman, Hayward, and Archer by surprise, along with the two thugs who had been in the limo with Archer. They stared at him, then Hayward's eyes shifted to the right. Tanner turned his head to see what the man was looking at when a rifle shot went off, the sound echoing off the cinder block walls.

Tanner fell to one knee while losing his grip on his weapon, which skittered away across the warehouse's concrete floor. The dark shirt Tanner wore grew darker near his right shoulder, and a stream of red flowed down his arm to drip off his fingertips.

Hayward raised a fist in the air. "Yes! You nailed him."

He was talking to the hit man he had hired. The man he'd been looking toward, and who had been concealed behind a stack of empty crates.

Tanner watched as the hit man walked over and picked up the weapon he'd dropped. The man pointed at him.

"Judging by the amount of blood he's losing, my shot

missed an artery, but he won't be using his gun arm for a while."

Steelman wore a knife in a leather sheath on his belt. He freed the long blade and held it out in front of him with his right hand.

Tanner stared at Hayward, then Steelman. "You want me dead; I get that. But before I die, tell me the truth. Who killed Tonya?"

Steelman said, "Who?"

"You never met her," Hayward said. "And I had nothing to do with her death either. If all this was really about you finding out who killed that girl, Tanner, then you've been wasting your time. However, you'll soon be able to ask Tonya herself who killed her... because you'll be dead too."

Steelman held his blade up so that it caught the light coming from the ceiling fixtures. "He's all mine. I'm gonna make him suffer, and then I'm gonna use this knife to saw his damn head off."

Hayward sighed. "You really are a tiresome brute. Do you know that, Steelman?"

Steelman glared at Hayward. "What the hell did you say to me?"

Hayward spoke to his hired gun. "You can kill him now."

The man freed a handgun and sent a round into Steelman's right knee. The biker howled, the knife clattered to the floor, and Hayward began shaking his head.

"Don't just wound him as you did Tanner. I want him dead."

The hit man laughed. "If he dies, it will be because Tanner killed him; I'm just here to help out."

"What?"

Tanner stood while reaching under his jacket. The two thugs standing near Archer went for their guns. One man had his holstered on his hip while the other had been holding a shotgun by its barrel with the stock resting on the ground. Hayward's hit man shot them both twice in the chest. One died immediately. The other, the man who'd had the shotgun, lay on his back moaning. The sound resonated with the moans coming from the wounded Steelman. A third shot to the chest put the man out of his misery.

Archer then made matters worse for the man by vomiting on him. Or maybe not, since the man was already dead.

Tanner hadn't been reaching for a weapon; he'd been removing the blood pack that had been used to make it appear that he'd been wounded. He had bought it at a theatrical supply store on Broadway. He tossed it on the floor, then held out his hand for his gun. Hayward's hit man handed it to him while smiling.

Hayward looked at Tanner, then at the man he had paid to kill him.

"What's going on?"

"Dude, Tanner and I go back years. Isn't that right, bro?"

"That's right, Romeo."

Archer, looking green, stumbled closer, while avoiding the blood from Steelman's leg wound.

"You two know each other?"

Romeo laughed. "Surprise!"

Archer looked offended. "You should have said something then. This is unethical."

"Sue me, dude."

Hayward held up his hands. "Okay. You outsmarted us. Congratulations. But don't you see? It can end here. You

154

now know that we weren't responsible for Tonya's death. No one else needs to die."

"I disagree," Tanner said. He shot Steelman in the head first, Hayward second, and then turned his weapon toward Archer.

The man was urinating on himself and was on the verge of passing out.

Tanner lowered his gun. "I'll let you live, Archer. But I'll need you to do something for me."

Archer's legs gave out, and he collapsed to the floor.

"Don't kill me. I'll do anything. Anything!"

"Yeah. I thought you'd say that."

23
THE CHOICE IS YOURS

RICHARD THAXTON RECEIVED A CALL FROM TANNER LATE at night and agreed to meet with him at his office. Tanner told him he had information that could prove his client's wife was murdered and had never had an affair with her younger assistant.

Thaxton arrived at the building where he kept his office. He used his key to unlock the outer door and waved to the old man, who worked as a security guard at night. He had called and let him know to expect him. There was a visitor waiting for him in the lobby. It wasn't Tanner. It was James Archer.

"Are you here to see me?"

"Is your name Richard Thaxton?"

"Yes."

"I'm James Archer. I'm here to see you. Tanner sent me here."

Thaxton had gotten closer to Archer. He wrinkled his nose as he caught the scent of urine.

Archer reddened from embarrassment. "I apologize for the way I smell. I-I had an accident earlier."

Thaxton nodded, then spoke to the security guard.

"This gentleman and I will be up in my office, Gary. Has anyone else been by?"

"Just ole pissy pants there," Gary said. The old man didn't like to mince words.

They took an elevator up to Thaxton's office in silence. Once inside, Thaxton turned on the lights in the outer office and started the coffee machine. His assistant always set it up before leaving for the day, in case Thaxton returned to the office late and wanted the brew. He definitely wanted it now, since it appeared he might be awake until the early morning hours, if not all night.

With the coffee brewing, he entered his own office. After putting on the lights, he went to a closet and removed a pair of gray sweatpants. There were times he'd feel like going for a run in the afternoon at a nearby park, so he kept the jogging clothes available. There were also sneakers and a matching gray sweatshirt.

Thaxton handed the sweatpants to Archer. "Change into these and toss those pants you're wearing into the trash bag that's lining the garbage can in my bathroom. You can change in there, and there's a washcloth and a towel so you can clean yourself too."

Red-faced again, Archer thanked Thaxton and entered the small powder room that was in a corner of the office.

Thaxton made himself a cup of coffee while he was waiting for Archer, added cream and sugar, then poured coffee into a second cup for his unexpected guest. After bringing the coffees into the office and setting them on the desk, Thaxton went back and grabbed the sugar dish and the container of light cream.

Archer left the bathroom with his body odor much improved but looked odd. He was wearing gray sweatpants with a blue dress shirt, red tie, and was carrying a black suit coat.

Thaxton gestured to the chairs in front of his desk, which he was settled behind.

"Have a seat, Mr. Archer. I'm very interested to hear what you have to tell me about the deaths of Fawna Davis and Scott Brown. And before you start, be advised that I'll be recording our conversation. I'll also be forwarding a copy of it to interested authorities."

Archer swallowed hard. "You mean the police?"

"Yes, and possibly the FBI."

Thaxton removed two tape recorders from a drawer, placed them on the desk, and hit their record buttons. He knew of a police detective who failed to record a murder confession when the tape recorder malfunctioned. Since learning of that incident, Thaxton always used two machines to record.

"Testing, 1,2,3."

He hit rewind on the digital devices, then their play buttons. His voice could be heard in stereo, clearly saying the words he'd just spoken. After hitting rewind on the machines again, he pressed the record buttons.

Thaxton identified himself by name and profession, noted the time, date, and place, then stated that a Mr. James Archer was with him and wished to make a declaration concerning the deaths of Fawna Davis and Scott Brown.

"You may begin your statement, Mr. Archer. Please start by stating your full name."

"Uh, I, um, my name is James Anthony Archer."

"Scott Brown was accused of murdering Fawna Davis before taking his own life. Do you have information that would dispute that?"

Archer said, "I…" and then he leapt from his seat and rushed out of the office.

"Mr. Archer! Please, come back!"

Archer rushed to the elevator, mashed the call button, and watched with relief as Thaxton was too late to reach him before the doors closed shut.

When he reached the lobby, he ran toward the exit. When he tried to open the door, he found it was locked. He called to the guard, Gary.

"Let me out of here!"

"Hold your horses," Gary said. The old man took his time getting to the door while taking out a set of keys. It was enough time for Thaxton to make it to the lobby on a different elevator.

"Mr. Archer. Please return to my office and speak to me. I won't record our conversation until you tell me you're ready to go on record."

"No. I need to get out of here. I can't go to prison, and that is what will happen if I reveal what I know."

Gary had unlocked the door. Archer flung it open, stepped outside, and took in a deep gulp of the night air. When he turned his head to the left, he spotted Tanner and Romeo staring at him.

"We had a deal, Archer," Tanner said. "Is this your way of telling me you'd rather die than tell the truth?"

Archer released a pitiful moan of despair. At that moment, he fully understood the old saying about being caught between a rock and a hard place. He either made a full statement about all the dirty deeds the black ops division had been involved with, or he would be dead before the sun came up.

Tears were in his eyes as he turned to reenter the building.

Two hours later, he had told Thaxton all he knew while being recorded.

THAXTON HAD ASKED MANY QUESTIONS DURING HIS interview of James Archer, but he had left a key one unasked.

Why?

Why confess your involvement in crimes that would certainly see you sentenced to spend many years behind bars?

He didn't need to ask that question because he knew the answer. Archer feared Tanner.

Thaxton had learned that sixteen members of a motorcycle club calling themselves Lucifer's Angels had been slaughtered by someone wielding a sniper rifle. That someone had been Tanner, and it was Tanner who had sent Archer to him.

Confess or die. That had been the choice Tanner had left Archer. Archer had decided to stay alive, even if it meant spending decades behind bars.

After shutting off the tape recorders, Thaxton was looking forward to calling his client in the morning and letting him know that his wife's good name had been restored. But first, there was another call he had to make.

BLUM'S VOICE WAS HOARSE FROM HAVING BEEN ASLEEP. "Who the hell is calling me in the middle of the night?"

"It's me, Colleen, Richard. I'm sorry to wake you, but you'll be glad I did."

"Richard? Is everything all right?"

Thaxton stared across his desk at Archer. The man was slumped in his seat and staring off into space while crying.

"I have a gift for you at my office. One that will help you restore a number of peoples' reputations and solve several homicides."

"What are you talking about?"

"You'll understand when you get here. And Colleen?"

"Yes?"

"You might get a promotion out of this. That's how big it is."

"I'll be right there."

2 4
ONE MORE

Heavy rain was in the forecast but had yet to materialize by the time Thaxton left the police station where Archer was being held. He had spent the morning at the precinct headquarters with Detective Blum and other police personnel.

He was asked why Archer chose him to confess to and he said the same thing Archer said, he had been chosen by Tanner, Tonya Wilson's mysterious boyfriend. When asked about his connection to Tanner, he told the truth, although he'd left out the detail of witnessing Tanner's abduction of Kevin and Kelly. Thaxton had spent more than a dozen years as a cop and his entire working life dealing with bad guys of one type or another. Tanner was a bad ass, a ruthless and efficient killer, but he wasn't a bad guy. Thaxton didn't think it would do anyone good for Tanner to be locked away in a cage for the crimes he committed. The man had been after revenge for the death of his woman, yes, but he'd also been an instrument of justice. By sparing Archer's life and making him confess his knowledge of crimes, Tanner had helped a lot of people and ended not one but two criminal enterprises. Lucifer's Angels were no more, and the same was true of Dangal Corps Black Ops Division.

Archer's confession about his involvement in the crimes the black ops unit committed helped to clear dozens of murder cases. Most of those murders had taken place over the last few days and had been committed by a man who was known by the single name of Tanner. Thaxton made sure it was officially noted that Tanner had been acting in self-defense in some instances.

Thaxton found that same Tanner approaching him as he returned to his office building. He sent him a smile.

"If I was still a cop, I'd slap handcuffs on you. But I'm not a cop, so I thank you for sending Archer to me. My client was very happy when I called him this morning, and their children will know their mother was an honorable woman."

"I'm glad I could help. Here are two more gifts."

Tanner had handed Thaxton the notebooks that Kevin and Kelly had written their confessions down in.

"Ah, excellent. The Doyle cousins' confessions likely match much of what Archer told me last night."

"Was there anything in his confession that would point to who killed Tonya Wilson?"

"I didn't notice anything. But come up to my office and I'll let you listen to it. I have my own copy."

"How long is the tape?"

"Just about two hours long."

"I don't want to spend that much time here; your cop friend might drop by."

"I left instructions for my assistant to make a transcript of it. If it's ready I'll give you a copy."

"That would work," Tanner said.

≈

THE TRANSCRIPT WAS READY. TANNER TOOK A COPY BACK to his hotel where he met with Romeo to have lunch together. Romeo's original contract in the United States was cancelled, but then Hayward contacted him through Archer and made an offer.

Romeo laughed aloud when he learned he was being hired to kill a man named Tanner, who was in New York City. James Archer had described Tanner as having "Scary eyes."

When Romeo phoned Tanner and gave him the news, the two of them came up with the plan to make Hayward believe he had won.

Tanner had been hoping the man would confess to having ordered Tonya's death through the motorcycle gang. Not only was that not the case, but Steelman had never heard of Tonya.

That meant Tonya's murderer was still out there.

≈

ROMEO WIPED HIS MOUTH WITH A NAPKIN AFTER EATING, then yawned. They were having lunch in a Chinese restaurant that was near their hotel and Romeo had been entertaining Tanner with stories about his life in Indonesia.

The rain had begun and was falling in a steady patter on the parked cars outside the window, making taxis hard to get, as few people were willing to walk in such weather.

"Oh man. Jet lag is kicking my butt; I need to get some sleep."

"What's her name?" Tanner said.

"What do you mean?"

"You seem as happy as I've ever seen you, Romeo. That usually means you're with someone special."

Romeo grinned. "You already know her."

Tanner smiled back at him. "Are you talking about Nadya?"

"Yeah dude. The little chick won my heart over. I'm in love with her."

They were drinking beer. Tanner held his glass up in a toast.

"Congratulations. I'm happy for you. My luck with love has been horrible. At least one of us should be lucky in love."

"You'll find someone someday, Cody. Were you in love with Tonya?"

"No. I liked her, and maybe it could have become something more, but I wasn't in love."

Romeo had yawned again. "I'm really sleepy, and this rainy weather is not helping. I'm gonna crash back at the hotel, then later we'll go out on the town, if you want."

"I'm not in the mood for barhopping, but I'll buy champagne to celebrate you and Nadya."

"Okay. What are you going to do while I'm sacked out?"

"I want to read the transcript of Archer's confession. Maybe I'll find something in it that will lead me to whoever killed Tonya."

"I wished I'd met her, man."

"So do I."

While Romeo caught up on his sleep, Tanner stayed awake and read. He wasn't feeling the effects of jet lag like Romeo, but he had been awake for more than twenty-four hours. He sipped on strong coffee as he read Thaxton's interview of Archer.

There was a part of it where Thaxton mentioned he had gotten a look at Michael Hallam's car, the vehicle that had struck and killed Tonya.

Tanner called him and asked him about it.

"Was there anything unusual?"

"Not really. But hold on. Detective Blum sent me an email about the car earlier. The Yonkers homicide detective who is handling Hallam's murder had their crime scene guys check it out. He was hoping there was a link between the hit-and-run and Hallam's murder."

Thaxton was quiet as he looked for the email. When he found it, he read the relevant information, then gave Tanner a summary of it.

"There was a tube of lip balm lying on the floor mats between the foot pedals, and a cigarette found in the ashtray was different from the type Hallam smoked."

"That means someone else could have been driving the car on the night Tonya was killed. Did they recover any fingerprints?"

"No. But they gathered DNA evidence off the cigarette. It will be some time before those results come back, although they have gotten quicker lately. Maybe the woman's DNA will be on file somewhere."

"A woman? Why are you so sure it was a woman driving the car?"

"I did sound certain, didn't I? Sorry. There's no proof it was a woman. I think I was making an assumption."

"Based on what, Thaxton?"

"Well, the lip balm. Sure, men use it too, but I'll bet you a lot more women use lip balm than men. And then there was the cigarette left in the ashtray."

"What about it?"

"It's a brand called Daisy. They advertise them as women's cigarettes, and they're slimmer and have a light pink tint to them."

There was silence on the line.

"Are you still there, Tanner?"

More silence.

"Tanner?"

"I'm here, but I have to go."

"Something I said struck a note with you, didn't it?"

"I have a question. That lip balm. What color was the tube it came in?"

"Um, pink. It was strawberry flavored."

"Thank you, Thaxton."

"You know who killed your girl, don't you?"

"I do. But I don't know why she did it."

The call ended. Thaxton thought about all the people Tanner had killed while searching for the truth about Tonya Wilson's death. He was certain there would soon be one more.

25
SMACKDOWN

Rae Houghton returned to her apartment to grab more boxes to take over to her new apartment. Her shitty new apartment was the way she thought about it, but it was all she could afford for now.

The rain was still coming down hard. She shook the moisture off her raincoat, so it landed out in the hallway instead of on her carpet. She sighed. No. It was no longer her carpet. She would be moving out for good in a few days.

She'd have to hire a moving company to transport her furniture, but it saved her a little money to move the smaller items herself.

She settled on her sofa with the cup of coffee she had bought from the expensive coffeehouse across the street. The four dollars she'd spent on the cappuccino was wasteful, but she was in the mood to treat herself. And besides, she had a reason to celebrate. Her plan had worked out.

She spilled some of the coffee when she heard a noise

come from behind her. After twisting her head around, she saw Tanner walking out of her bedroom.

"What the hell are you doing in my apartment, Tanner?"

He held up a garment that belonged to her. It was a yellow hoodie. "I was looking for this."

"What are you talking about?"

"You were wearing this jacket on the night you ran Tonya over with Michael Hallam's car. Hallam's neighbor saw you wearing it from across the street on the day you killed him too. The girl described you as being a tall man who was slim. It never occurred to her that a woman could be your height. What are you, five-foot-eleven?"

"Five-foot-eleven-and a half," Rae said, as she scooted forward on the sofa. She sprang off it an instant later and ripped open the drawer on the table that was near her locked door. Her hand searched frantically for something that was no longer there.

Tanner reached behind his back and removed the gun he had taken from the drawer earlier. He had been inside Rae's apartment for over an hour.

He held up the gun. "I have your weapon. Go sit back on the couch."

"I can explain. Will you let me explain?"

"I said sit down."

Rae returned to the couch and sat. She was watching Tanner as if he were a rattlesnake about to strike, knowing he was every bit as deadly as a rattler.

Tanner settled beside her. "Let's hear it. Why did you kill Tonya?"

"Be-because of you."

"What does that mean?"

"That day I ran into you and Tonya, I was with a guy named Manny. Remember?"

"I remember. So what?"

"You don't know Manny, but Manny knew about you. Manny is a mob guy, Tanner. He said he'd seen you hanging out with some other mob guy named Joe, and that you were a hit man."

"Why did you kill Tonya, Rae? That's all I want to know."

Rae wiped at her eyes. "I wanted revenge."

"Against Tonya?"

"No. I had nothing against Tonya. I wanted revenge on Brent Hayward and that asshole, Steelman."

Tanner stared at her, and then he noticed the upside-down triangle that was colored red, and that he had seen before. It was a tattoo of some type on Rae's arm. The rest of it was hidden by her long sleeve. He grabbed her by the arm and she shrieked. When Tanner moved her sleeve up, he saw a tattoo displaying a red, grinning Devil's head, the logo of Lucifer's Angels. The upside-down, red triangle was one of two Devil horns.

Tanner saw the whole thing then and understood. He had been used unwittingly as an instrument of vengeance. And Tonya was murdered to set Rae's evil scheme in motion. She had died for nothing.

"You were the one who introduced Hayward to Steelman?"

"Yes. I was told I would get a percentage of everything Steelman was paid. That was a lie; he kept it all for himself. When I complained to Hayward, the son of a bitch framed me for theft of company property and fired me."

"Steelman was with a girl who couldn't have been more than eighteen. Was she your replacement?"

Rae's face twisted with hate. "That little bitch, Shawna. She's seventeen. I was only sixteen the first time Steelman and I hooked up. The bastard said I was getting old. Old? I'm twenty-five." The anger left her face, and she smiled. "He's dead now, and so is Brent Hayward. It was on the news that their bodies were found down by the docks."

"Yes. Your plan worked. You knew I would think Hayward or Steelman had something to do with Tonya's death, and that I would kill them for killing her. But they didn't kill her, Rae. You killed her." Tanner pointed to a pink cap that was lying on top of her marble coffee table. It was beside an empty pack of cigarettes. The brand name on the cigarettes was Daisy.

"That's the top from a tube of strawberry lip balm. You lost the bottom part of it in Michael Hallam's car. You also left behind a cigarette you had smoked. The cops have your DNA."

"They won't be able to match it with anything. I've never been arrested."

"And you never will be."

Rae's breathing increased, as she understood Tanner's meaning. She held up a hand.

"Before you shoot me, listen to me. It was wrong of me to use Tonya to make you go after Hayward and Steelman. You're mad about that, I get it, but I have a reason to be mad too."

"Let me hear your reason."

"You killed my friends, Tanner. I wanted Steelman dead, yeah, but not the whole damn motorcycle club. Those people were my friends."

"They're dead because of you, Rae. You wanted me to seek vengeance; you got it. Do you have any more excuses?"

"I-I…" She smiled. "Killing me would be a waste. I mean, look at me. I'm not curvy like Tonya was, but I'm all woman, and I know how to please a man in bed. Let me live, and I'll make you so happy. I swear I will."

Rae flinched as Tanner raised a hand, but then she relaxed when he reached behind her to caress her long blonde hair. At least, she thought he had been caressing it. He hadn't. He'd been gathering a fistful of it to get a good grip on her.

"Tonya loved me, Rae, and you killed her."

Tanner slammed her head forward and her face smashed against the marble coffee table. When he lifted her head up, blood was flowing from her broken nose and her bottom lip was split open.

"No, Tanner... don't."

He slammed her head down again, brought her back up, and did it again. Her body went limp after the fourth impact, but he kept smashing her head against her beloved Carrara marble table until it cracked her evil skull open. The table's white surface was turning red and was littered with bits of broken teeth.

Tanner released her when he was certain she was dead and left her apartment with blood streaking his face and clothing.

The rain was still coming down in sheets, just as it had been on the night Tonya was murdered. It washed away the evidence of Rae's death, but nothing would ever cleanse the memory of her heartlessness from Tanner, or the feeling of loss whenever he thought of Tonya.

Tanner walked along in the rain, alone again.

EPILOGUE

Miles Peterson entered the MegaZenith Building and headed up to the top floor of the sixty-story office building. He had news to tell his boss, Frank Richards.

As Richards' right-hand man, Peterson was able to bypass speaking to Richards' personal assistant and walked past her to knock on the office door.

He heard Richards yell the word, "Enter!" and went inside. He had been hoping to find him alone. Instead, that pesky intern, Al Trent, was in the office. Then Peterson remembered that Trent was no longer an intern and was working full time. He'd been given a choice position as a junior executive. It had taken Peterson years of work to reach that level. At forty-five, he considered a teenager like Trent to be nothing more than an upstart punk.

Trent was nerdy but thought himself superior because he'd been gifted with a high intellect. He had graduated from Harvard at only nineteen and made sure everyone knew it.

Peterson was holding a folded copy of a newspaper, The Business Times, he held it up and addressed Richards.

"I need to speak to you in private, sir."

Al Trent rose from his seat and smiled at Peterson. "It's good to see you again, Mr. Peterson."

When Peterson said nothing, Trent said goodbye to Richards and left the office.

"Why were you rude to Al, Miles?"

"I don't like that kid. And I think he wants my job."

"And he'll have it someday the way he's going. He closed the deal with Seavers Enterprises today. Jack Seavers has agreed verbally to sell us his company."

"What? I thought that deal was dead in the water?"

"It was until Al revived it. He went to school with Jack Seavers' son, and the boy gave Al a chance to talk with his father. Trent talked to the man for three hours, and the deal he came up with was better than what we originally wanted."

"It was damn presumptuous of him to discuss company business he wasn't authorized to perform."

"The deal was dead. There was nothing to lose and everything to gain. Al Trent is going places, Miles; you might want to keep that in mind."

Peterson shook his head in irritation as he unfolded the newspaper he was carrying. He laid it on Richards' desk.

"Have you seen this?"

Richards pointed to a television that was on the wall to the right of his desk.

"I saw a report of it on the news. Dangal Corp. is under investigation by three federal agencies and will end up paying a massive fine for what the media is calling their Black Ops Division."

"In the newspaper story, they're reporting that Brent Hayward was behind the whole thing."

"And was killed when he lost control of it."

"The man had formed an alliance with a motorcycle gang. What the hell could he have been thinking?"

"His thinking was fine. It was his execution of the idea that was flawed. Instead of forming an alliance with a motorcycle gang with limited resources and experience, he should have reached out to a top man in the criminal world."

Peterson blinked at his boss in surprise. "You believe his plan had merit?"

"I do, and it has caused me to think in new ways. Imagine it, Miles. To not only rule the legitimate business world, to also wield the sort of power a mafia Don has. People respect us, but they don't fear us, and fear is a power all its own."

Peterson leaned back in his chair. "Forming an association with the mafia would be risky, but yes, I can see advantages. They can get away with things we never could."

"And we could offer them a cloak of respectability to hide behind. Besides, the way the world is heading, business practices have been becoming more criminal for decades, while criminal organizations often own legitimate enterprises to convert their ill-gotten gains into explainable income. A merger between business and the criminal world seems inevitable."

Peterson laughed. "You're really considering doing this?"

Richards waved a hand in the air. "For now, it's still an idea, one I'd like you to explore. Find out what you can about the players on the other side. I'll want to know as much about them as I can before I make a decision."

"If you were to bring about this... association, this conglomerate. You would become one of the most powerful men in the world, along with whoever you partnered with, of course."

"Any partnership would be ended once I gained control. After that, the power would be all mine."

Peterson stood. "I'll begin researching this and have a report for you by the end of the week."

"Yes. Do that."

Peterson left the office. Frank Richards stood and turned to look out the wide window behind his desk. Sunlight glinted off his graying hair as he took in the impressive view of the Manhattan skyline.

Frank Richards was a powerful and influential man, but power came in many forms. He found the type of power created by fear to be seductive. The people working under him kowtowed to him and dreaded displeasing him because it could mean the end of their employment. What would it be like to have men fear you because they knew you could end their lives on a mere whim? That was power. It was a form of power Frank Richards craved.

Yes, Brent Hayward had the right idea, but his approach and handling of it left much to be desired.

"I would do things right," Richards said to himself, and the idea grew ever more enticing to him.

TANNER RETURNS!

THE NEW THING - TANNER 52

AFTERWORD

Thank you,

REMINGTON KANE

GET FREE BOOKS!

You'll receive FREE books, such as,

SLAY BELLS – A TANNER NOVEL – BOOK 0

TAKEN! ALPHABET SERIES – 26 ORIGINAL TAKEN! TALES

BLUE STEELE - KARMA

Also – Exclusive short stories featuring TANNER, along with other books.

TO BECOME A MAILING LIST MEMBER, GO TO:
    http://remingtonkane.com/mailing-list/

ALSO BY REMINGTON KANE

The TANNER Series in order

INEVITABLE I - A Tanner Novel - Book 1

KILL IN PLAIN SIGHT - A Tanner Novel - Book 2

MAKING A KILLING ON WALL STREET - A Tanner Novel - Book 3

THE FIRST ONE TO DIE LOSES - A Tanner Novel - Book 4

THE LIFE & DEATH OF CODY PARKER - A Tanner Novel - Book 5

WAR - A Tanner Novel- A Tanner Novel - Book 6

SUICIDE OR DEATH - A Tanner Novel - Book 7

TWO FOR THE KILL - A Tanner Novel - Book 8

BALLET OF DEATH - A Tanner Novel - Book 9

MORE DANGEROUS THAN MAN - A Tanner Novel - Book 10

TANNER TIMES TWO - A Tanner Novel - Book 11

OCCUPATION: DEATH - A Tanner Novel - Book 12

HELL FOR HIRE - A Tanner Novel - Book 13

A HOME TO DIE FOR - A Tanner Novel - Book 14

FIRE WITH FIRE - A Tanner Novel - Book 15

TO KILL A KILLER - A Tanner Novel - Book 16

WHITE HELL – A Tanner Novel - Book 17

MANHATTAN HIT MAN – A Tanner Novel - Book 18

ONE HUNDRED YEARS OF TANNER – A Tanner Novel - Book 19

REVELATIONS - A Tanner Novel - Book 20

THE SPY GAME - A Tanner Novel - Book 21

A VICTIM OF CIRCUMSTANCE - A Tanner Novel - Book 22

A MAN OF RESPECT - A Tanner Novel - Book 23

THE MAN, THE MYTH - A Tanner Novel - Book 24

ALL-OUT WAR - A Tanner Novel - Book 25

THE REAL DEAL - A Tanner Novel - Book 26

WAR ZONE - A Tanner Novel - Book 27

ULTIMATE ASSASSIN - A Tanner Novel - Book 28

KNIGHT TIME - A Tanner Novel - Book 29

PROTECTOR - A Tanner Novel - Book 30

BULLETS BEFORE BREAKFAST - A Tanner Novel - Book 31

VENGEANCE - A Tanner Novel - Book 32

TARGET: TANNER - A Tanner Novel - Book 33

BLACK SHEEP - A Tanner Novel - Book 34

FLESH AND BLOOD - A Tanner Novel - Book 35

NEVER SEE IT COMING - A Tanner Novel - Book 36

MISSING - A Tanner Novel - Book 37

CONTENDER - A Tanner Novel - Book 38

TO SERVE AND PROTECT - A Tanner Novel - Book 39

STALKING HORSE - A Tanner Novel - Book 40

THE EVIL OF TWO LESSERS - A Tanner Novel - Book 41

SINS OF THE FATHER AND MOTHER - A Tanner Novel - Book 42

SOULLESS - A Tanner Novel - Book 43

LIT FUSE - A Tanner Novel - Book 44

HYENAS - A Tanner Novel - Book 45

MANHUNT - A Tanner Novel - Book 46

IN FOR THE KILL - A Tanner Novel - Book 47

RESURRECTION - A Tanner Novel - Book 48

ASSASSIN'S DELIGHT - A Tanner Novel - Book 49

DOUBLE DEAD - A Tanner Novel - Book 50

GHOSTS FROM THE PAST - A Tanner Novel - Book 51

THE NEW THING - A Tanner Novel - 52

The Young Guns Series in order
YOUNG GUNS

YOUNG GUNS 2 - SMOKE & MIRRORS

YOUNG GUNS 3 - BEYOND LIMITS

YOUNG GUNS 4 - RYKER'S RAIDERS

YOUNG GUNS 5 - ULTIMATE TRAINING

YOUNG GUNS 6 - CONTRACT TO KILL

YOUNG GUNS 7 - FIRST LOVE

YOUNG GUNS 8 - THE END OF THE BEGINNING

A Tanner Series in order
TANNER: YEAR ONE

TANNER: YEAR TWO

TANNER: YEAR THREE

TANNER: YEAR FOUR

TANNER: YEAR FIVE

TANNER: YEAR SIX

TANNER: YEAR SEVEN

TANNER: YEAR EIGHT

The TAKEN! Series in order

TAKEN! - LOVE CONQUERS ALL - Book 1

TAKEN! - SECRETS & LIES - Book 2

TAKEN! - STALKER - Book 3

TAKEN! - BREAKOUT! - Book 4

TAKEN! - THE THIRTY-NINE - Book 5

TAKEN! - KIDNAPPING THE DEVIL - Book 6

TAKEN! - HIT SQUAD - Book 7

TAKEN! - MASQUERADE - Book 8

TAKEN! - SERIOUS BUSINESS - Book 9

TAKEN! - THE COUPLE THAT SLAYS TOGETHER - Book 10

TAKEN! - PUT ASUNDER - Book 11

TAKEN! - LIKE BOND, ONLY BETTER - Book 12

TAKEN! - MEDIEVAL - Book 13

TAKEN! - RISEN! - Book 14

TAKEN! - VACATION - Book 15

TAKEN! - MICHAEL - Book 16

TAKEN! - BEDEVILED - Book 17

TAKEN! - INTENTIONAL ACTS OF VIOLENCE - Book 18

TAKEN! - THE KING OF KILLERS – Book 19

TAKEN! - NO MORE MR. NICE GUY - Book 20 & the Series Finale

The MR. WHITE Series

PAST IMPERFECT - MR. WHITE - Book 1

HUNTED - MR. WHITE - Book 2

SOVEREIGN - MR. WHITE - Book 3

The UNLEASH Series

TERROR IN NEW YORK - Book 1

THE EXECUTIONER'S MASK - Book 2

THE XANDER PLAGUE - Book 3

The BLUE STEELE Series in order

BLUE STEELE - BOUNTY HUNTER- Book 1

BLUE STEELE - BROKEN- Book 2

BLUE STEELE - VENGEANCE- Book 3

BLUE STEELE - THAT WHICH DOESN'T KILL ME- Book 4

BLUE STEELE - ON THE HUNT- Book 5

BLUE STEELE - PAST SINS - Book 6

BLUE STEELE - DADDY'S GIRL - Book 7 & the Series Finale

The CALIBER DETECTIVE AGENCY Series in order

CALIBER DETECTIVE AGENCY - GENERATIONS- Book 1

CALIBER DETECTIVE AGENCY - TEMPTATION- Book 2

CALIBER DETECTIVE AGENCY - A RANSOM PAID IN BLOOD- Book 3

CALIBER DETECTIVE AGENCY - MISSING- Book 4

CALIBER DETECTIVE AGENCY - DECEPTION- Book 5

CALIBER DETECTIVE AGENCY - CRUCIBLE- Book 6

CALIBER DETECTIVE AGENCY – LEGENDARY – Book 7

CALIBER DETECTIVE AGENCY – WE ARE GATHERED HERE TODAY - Book 8

CALIBER DETECTIVE AGENCY - MEANS, MOTIVE, and OPPORTUNITY - Book 9 & the Series Finale

THE TAKEN!/TANNER Series in order

THE CONTRACT: KILL JESSICA WHITE - Taken!/Tanner - Book 1

UNFINISHED BUSINESS – Taken!/Tanner – Book 2

THE ABDUCTION OF THOMAS LAWSON - Taken!/Tanner – Book 3

PREDATOR - Taken!/Tanner - Book 4

DETECTIVE PIERCE Series in order

MONSTERS - A Detective Pierce Novel - Book 1

DEMONS - A Detective Pierce Novel - Book 2

ANGELS - A Detective Pierce Novel - Book 3

THE OCEAN BEACH ISLAND Series in order

THE MANY AND THE ONE - Book 1

SINS & SECOND CHANES - Book 2

DRY ADULTERY, WET AMBITION -Book 3

OF TONGUE AND PEN - Book 4

ALL GOOD THINGS… - Book 5

LITTLE WHITE SINS - Book 6

THE LIGHT OF DARKNESS - Book 7

STERN ISLAND - Book 8 & the Series Finale

THE REVENGE Series in order

JOHNNY REVENGE - The Revenge Series - Book 1

THE APPOINTMENT KILLER - The Revenge Series - Book 2

AN I FOR AN I - The Revenge Series - Book 3

POETRY

DIFFERENT FLESH, ON DIFFERENT BONES

LIKE A SOUL, MOLESTED

NONFICTION

INDIE: A Humorous Look at Independent Publishing

ALSO

THE EFFECT: Reality is changing!

THE FIX-IT MAN: A Tale of True Love and Revenge

DOUBLE OR NOTHING

PARKER & KNIGHT

REDEMPTION: Someone's taken her

DESOLATION LAKE

TIME TRAVEL TALES & OTHER SHORT STORIES